Countdown to New Beginnings

Dianna Houx

Contents

Reading Order

1.) Countdown to Christmas
2.) Countdown to Valentine's Day
3.) Countdown to Easter
4.) Countdown to Mother's Day
5.) Countdown to 4th of July!
6.) Countdown to Halloween!
7.) Countdown to Thanksgiving!
8.) Countdown to Christmas Eve!
9.) Countdown to New Beginnings
10.) Countdown to a Wedding

I recommend reading the books in order. There is an overarching storyline that starts in book 1 and continues throughout the series. Plus, it's more fun that way!

-Days till New Years-

Six-Morning

'Twas the morning after Christmas and all through the house, everyone was stirring—there was chaos in the boardinghouse!

Grace chuckled at her little rhyme as she made her way downstairs to help prepare breakfast. Her Christmas guests were busy preparing to head home, and there were boxes, suitcases, and various other items lining the hallway as she passed. She could hear mumbled voices from behind doors, mixed with the cries of babies and the squeals of Leo and Leora, teenage twins, as they fought over whose turn it was to play their new video game. Grace did not envy their parents and their long car ride back to the city.

Usually, the morning guests checked out were bittersweet, but since she was going from one group of guests to the next, Grace didn't have the luxury this time of feeling sad as she said goodbye to the people she had just spent the biggest holiday of the year with. In some ways, they felt like family. In others, she knew it was unlikely she would see most of them again.

A small sigh escaped her lips as she joined Jilly in the kitchen. "What can I do to help?" Grace asked her friend.

Jilly looked at Grace, her eyes wide as she brushed bits of gluten-free flour off her cheeks before picking up her whisk and furiously mixing what looked like pancake batter. "Eggs! We need eggs!"

Grace gently pried the whisk and bowl from Jilly's hands and set them on the counter. "Are you okay?"

"I got about three hours of sleep last night and am on my fifth cup of coffee," Jilly replied, her hands shaking now that they no longer held something to steady them. "I might be a little jittery," she said sheepishly.

That felt like an understatement, but Grace didn't have the heart to say that. Still, she was very concerned. She'd only known Jilly for a few months, but in that short amount of time, Jilly had always appeared calm and in control, even when things were falling apart around them. Seeing her like this was not only disconcerting, it was alarming.

"Did something happen with your in-laws?" Grace asked quietly.

Jilly shook her head. "While I can see why you would think that, I still haven't heard from them since Thanksgiving. They didn't even call the kids on Christmas, opting to send a box of presents instead. Which is honestly scarier than if they had demanded to see them for the holiday. I don't know what is going on with them, but whatever it is, it must be big."

"So, you still think they're going to come after you for custody?" The thought was still so shocking, Grace could barely get the words out without tripping over them.

"Yes, I do," Jilly nodded emphatically. "Which is why I've been spending every free moment I have on trying to figure out a plan. And why I'm living on practically no sleep and way too much caffeine."

Grace walked over to the fridge and pulled out a sixty-count box of eggs. She then grabbed a pan from the cupboard, set it on the stove, and began to crack eggs as she talked. "I'd ask if there's anything I can do to help, but I'm sure the answer to that hasn't changed since the last time I asked."

"No, but my appreciation remains the same." Jilly turned to face Grace and began to fidget with the strings of her apron. "Um, I hate to do this to you, but..."

A sense of foreboding overcame Grace and startled her so badly she dropped an uncracked egg into the pan. "You're about to tell me you can't help out today, aren't you?" she asked, as a sense of panic joined the foreboding.

Jilly grimaced, opened her mouth to respond, then quickly shut it as the guests filed into the room for breakfast. "We'll talk later," she mouthed to Grace.

Visions of her to-do list danced through Grace's head as she tried to concentrate on serving her guests. Was it possible to get everything done without Jilly? She wasn't sure, but she would have to try. What other choice did she have?

"Good morning, Grace."

Grace looked up to see Grant standing in front of her. She hadn't seen him come in, and when she saw the haggard look on his face, she immediately searched the room for Molly. When she didn't see her, Grace turned her attention back to Grant, concern forming a pit in her already agitated stomach.

"What's wrong?" Grace squeaked out. "Is it Eliza? Is she okay?"

Grant sighed. "Eliza has a cold. According to the nurse, whom Molly has called at least a dozen times since last night, it's not serious, but that has done little to reassure Mama Bear."

Jilly chuckled as she flipped another pancake. "I remember the first time my oldest got sick. You would have thought the world was ending the way I carried on." She gave Grant a reassuring smile. "You will get through this, I promise."

He cleared his throat. "Thank you, I have no doubt that you're right. However," he adjusted his necktie nervously, "Molly is refusing to leave the house until Eliza's better."

"Oh, well, in that case, let me make you a couple of plates to go," Jilly volunteered.

Normally, that would have been something Grace offered to do, but she was too busy staring off into space as the true meaning of Grant's words dawned on her: Molly would not be available to help over the next few days. She hated that Eliza was sick and felt a lot of empathy for Molly, but it was not easy to overlook how her friends kept getting her into these difficult situations and then left her to figure out how to deal with them on her own.

"I'm sorry," Grant said, interrupting Grace's train of thought. "I know this isn't fair to you."

Grace waved him off and tried to smile. "It's fine. These things happen." She added eggs to the plates Jilly was assembling as she tried to convince herself that her words were true. Somehow, everything would be okay.

As Jilly bagged up the plates, Grace poured coffee into travel cups and then handed them to Grant. "I'll try to stop by later and check on Molly and the baby."

"Perhaps a text would be best." Grant winced. "Molly doesn't want anyone around the baby right now in case they have germs or something."

"That's probably for the best," Grace agreed.

Grant nodded, then thanked them for the food. "I know she'll appreciate this," he said, gesturing toward the cups and plates.

Grace watched as Grant moved toward the door. They'd spent enough time talking; the guests had finished eating and were now milling about as they prepared to leave for the final time. She checked her watch and saw it was eight-thirty; if everyone left by nine-thirty, she'd have just enough time to get to the hotel and do a final once-over before the new guests began to arrive.

"I'll try to get breakfast cleaned up before I leave," Jilly assured Grace.

That would make for one less thing Grace had to do, but she could tell from the tone of Jilly's voice she really didn't have the time. "It's okay, I'll take care of it," Grace told her.

Jilly shook her head. "I'm really sorry, Grace, I hate that I'm letting you down. It's just, we only have a couple of days until the banks are closed again for the next holiday, and Bea and I are trying to do as much as we can to transfer ownership before the end of the year. Then I have to try to find a house to rent, and—"

Grace reached out and put a comforting hand on Jilly's shoulder. "Honestly, it's okay," she said gently. "I truly appreciate all the help you've given me—I mean really appreciate it—but you have to do what's best for you and the kids. So please, don't worry about me, I'll figure things out."

Tears streaked down Jilly's face as she hugged Grace. "Thank you. If we finish early, I promise to come back and get some cleaning done." She pulled back, took off her apron, then did her best to paste a smile on. "Wish me luck? I'm about to be the proud owner of a bakery!"

"I wish you nothing but happiness and success!" Grace hugged Jilly one last time. "Now go and make it official, I've got things under control." As soon as Jilly was gone, Grace turned her attention back to her guests. Megan and Ross were the first to leave, though since they didn't have kids to wrangle, that wasn't much of a surprise.

"Thanks, Grace," Megan said as she hugged Grace goodbye. "We had so much fun, we might have to make this a tradition!"

Grace returned the hug, then turned to shake Ross's hand. "I would love to have you back, anytime!"

They moved to the porch, where Grace took a moment to study the sky while the couple loaded their luggage into the trunk of their car. She was no weather expert, but it looked like snow was in their future—which was honestly the last thing she needed right now, but she had a feeling she wasn't going to get a vote.

As soon as Megan and Ross pulled out of the driveway, Grace waved goodbye, then went back inside where she found Arnie and Louisa exchanging phone numbers with Teddy and Hannah. Grace couldn't help but smile at the new friendships that had formed between her guests. Bringing people together was her favorite part of running a B&B.

"It looks like everyone is ready to go!" Grace exclaimed. She inwardly winced as soon as the words were out of her mouth. Did that sound like she was pushing them out the door? In a way, she kind of was, but she didn't want them to know that.

"We actually are ready," Teddy replied with a laugh. "Getting the five of us out the door on time might just be a Christmas miracle!"

Hannah rolled her eyes and smacked her husband on the arm playfully. "The real miracle will be keeping those two from fighting all the way home," she said, motioning toward the twins, Leo and Leora.

All eyes turned toward the duo, who were so engrossed in the video game Leo was playing they had completely tuned out all the adults around them.

Arnie nudged Louisa with his elbow. "That might be a reason to stop at one!"

"Don't let their bickering fool you," Hannah replied. "Those two are the best of friends!" She looked at her youngest, Lexi, who was snuggled up in her car seat, then back to Arnie. "And as you can see, we didn't even stop at two!"

Their banter was amusing, but Grace had a schedule to stick to, and she really needed them to get on the road.

"Can I get anyone anything before you go?" she asked the group. "Perhaps a drink or snack for the trip home?"

"Can we have hot chocolate?" Leo and Leora asked, their eyes still glued to the game.

Grace looked to Hannah, and when she nodded, quickly made her way over to the breakfast bar and fixed a couple of to-go cups for the kids.

"Anyone else?" Grace asked as she handed the cups to the twins. When no one else responded, she stepped back and assessed the situation. "How about some help carrying luggage to your cars?"

"That would be great!" Hannah said enthusiastically. She pointed to the large pile of suitcases, baby gear, and bags and boxes that had been piled haphazardly by the door. "We have to find a way to squeeze all of that into the trunk."

Judging by the size of the heap, that might require an additional Christmas miracle, but Grace was up to the challenge. So, she grabbed as many bags as she could and followed Teddy out to their SUV, where she spent the next fifteen minutes playing Tetris as she tried to shimmy and squeeze as much as she could into the trunk. When that was done, she gave them all a quick hug, then waved goodbye as she hurried back to the house to help Arnie and Louisa—only, they were nowhere to be found.

"If you're looking for the other couple, they said to tell you goodbye," Carl said as he appeared in the doorway to the dining room.

"Oh," Grace said, unable to hide her disappointment. It would have been nice to say a proper goodbye, especially since it was rare she ever saw her guests again.

"Don't look so dejected," Carl said as he gave her a hug. "They knew you were busy with Hannah and Teddy and didn't want to bother you."

They probably also picked up on Grace's attempts to practically shove them out the door. With her luck, she'd offended them and they would leave a bad review for the B&B as soon as they got home. Or maybe she was being dramatic again and allowing her stress to conjure up nothing but worst-case scenarios. Time would tell.

"You don't have to leave," Grace said to Carl, changing the subject. "I know we haven't set a new date for the wedding, but I'm still hopeful it will be sometime this century!"

Katherine entered the room, took one look at the dishes scattered all over the table, the dirty pots and pans in the kitchen sink, and the leftover food still sitting out on the breakfast bar. "We could stay long enough to help get this place in order," she offered.

"That is not what I meant when I said you could stay," Grace protested. "I'm just sad to see you leave again so soon. It feels like I barely had any time to spend with you two."

"We'll be back as soon as you give us a date for the wedding," Katherine replied. "For now, Carl and I are going to take advantage of the beautiful Arizona weather and go see the Grand Canyon!"

It was hard to compete with that. And if she were honest, even if they did stay, Grace still wouldn't have time to spend with them. At least not for the next seven days. It really was for the best they went out and had fun.

"I'll miss you both," she said, hugging each of them in turn.

"And we will miss you!" Carl said, returning her hug. "Someday you guys will have to visit us in The Big Easy! We'll give you a proper tour of New Orleans, ghosts and all!"

Grace smiled, her first real smile of the morning, at the thought of going on vacation to visit her friends. "I'm going to take you up on that!"

"We will, too," Granny and Gladys said in unison as they entered the dining room from the living area.

They looked so happy, Grace vowed then and there to make this a reality as soon as possible. She just had to get through this next week. And her wedding. And whatever else life threw her way.

After many more hugs and promises to send pictures of their travels, Katherine and Carl left. Grace then looked at her watch and grimaced: nine-forty-five. Her window for getting to the hotel and preparing before the new guests arrived was quickly closing.

"I promise to get this place cleaned up as soon as I get back," Grace promised as she gave Granny a quick hug. "Is there anything I can get you two before I leave?"

"We'll be fine, dear," Granny assured her.

Grace looked at her just in time to catch the look Granny and Gladys exchanged. They were disappointed in her. If she were honest, she was disappointed, too. In all the years she'd been taking care of this house, she had never left it in such a state of disarray. But there simply wasn't time to deal with it now, so she would have to make it up to Granny later.

"Love you both," Grace said, before grabbing her purse and bolting out the door. Surely one day of dirty dishes wouldn't hurt anyone. Right?

Six-Afternoon

It was five minutes to ten when Grace pulled into the parking lot of the hotel. To her utter dismay, despite there still being an hour until check-in, there was a car already parked by the front door. There went her plans for a last-minute walk-through. At this point, she had no choice but to hope she and Jilly had covered all the bases when they'd been there a few days ago.

With a sigh, Grace got out of the car and hurried to open the door. It wasn't her fault a guest had arrived early, but that didn't mean she wanted to keep them waiting. First impressions had a way of setting the tone for the 'Experience,' and she wanted to make a good one.

"Grace, hold on!"

Surprised, Grace turned to see Linda, from Rustic Petals and Posies, exiting her car.

"Oh my gosh, Linda!" Grace exclaimed, her hand going to her heart. "I completely forgot I was supposed to meet you here. I'm so sorry!"

"No worries," Linda replied, waving a hand dismissively. "If you've got a free hand, I have the bouquets you ordered." She walked to the back of her car and opened the trunk, revealing a large floral arrangement consisting of white roses with black and gold accents and a large 'Happy 50th Anniversary' sign displayed prominently amongst the display. In addition to that were a handful of smaller bouquets Grace could use to adorn the center of the tables in the dining room, as well as the side tables in the lobby.

"You've really outdone yourself," Grace said, a tinge of awe in her voice. As she stared at Linda's hard work, a rare moment of gratitude came over her that her wedding had been postponed: allowing time for Linda to work her magic on the flowers for the wedding would not be a hardship.

HONK

They both turned to see a towns-person waving through their car window as they drove by. Grace couldn't see who it was, nor did she know if the person was waving to her or Linda, but she waved back anyway. Then she snapped back to reality, the looming pressure from the literal and proverbial ticking clock once again overcoming her. She needed to move—and fast—if she was going to get the bouquets in place before the first guest arrived.

Thirty minutes later, Grace placed the last bouquet on the front desk of the lobby. Did she really need to take thirty minutes to place a handful of floral arrangements around the hotel? No, but she couldn't seem to stop obsessing over the small things. What was that saying—the devil is in the details? Or was that really just an excuse to procrastinate? Given the amount of work on her to-do list, she had a feeling it was the latter. Worse than that, now that she thought about it, how was she even supposed to get the items on her to-do list done? It wasn't possible to be in two places at once, so how was she supposed to check the guests in and prepare lunch? Or dinner? Or run around handing out the extra blankets, pillows, and towels her guests inevitably ask for?

As the overwhelming thoughts swirled around in her head, Grace slumped forward on the desk, her face in her hands. "How do I keep getting into these situations?" she groaned.

The little bell over the entrance jingled, signaling the arrival of a guest. With a start, Grace popped her head up and pasted a smile on her face, then sighed when she saw who it was.

"You look like you're on the verge of a breakdown," Lyda said as she studied Grace. Concern replaced her curiosity as she approached the front desk.

"I feel like I'm on the verge of a breakdown," Grace admitted. She was surprised by how quickly she'd voiced that out loud. Discussing negative feelings was still something she struggled with, especially in front of people like Lyda, who always seemed to have it together.

Lyda leaned her elbows on the desk and nodded sharply. "What can I do to help?"

Grace exhaled as she shook her head. "Honestly, I don't even know anymore. The house is a disaster, which I guess isn't terrible since no one is staying there, but still, it's on my mind. There are fifty-two guests scheduled to check in at any moment, so someone has to man the front desk, but someone also has to prepare lunch, dinner, dessert, snacks, and deal with any requests the guests might make." She paused to take a breath, her eyes closing as she mentally studied her list. "Molly is at home with a sick baby, Rebekah is at the winery working to get it ready for the big party on New Year's Eve, and Jilly is busy signing paperwork for the bakery."

"Which leaves you to do the work of at least three people?" Lyda asked, her brow raised.

"I can't do it all," Grace whispered as panic rose in her chest. She looked at Lyda as tears spilled down her cheeks. She couldn't remember the last time she had felt this helpless.

Lyda reached over and gently patted Grace's hand. "Take a deep breath," she commanded. She demonstrated a breathing technique, then waited patiently for Grace to calm down. Once Lyda felt confident Grace's panic attack had subsided, she resumed. "I'm not much of a cook, but I am good with administrative work, so how about this—I'll take over here, and you go get started on lunch?"

Grace had never wanted to take someone up on an offer as badly as she wanted to right now, but could she really impose on her new friend like that?

"Are you sure?" Grace grimaced at the sound of her voice—it reeked of desperation. "I doubt playing hotel concierge was on your list of things to do today." She attempted a little laugh to lighten the mood but could tell by Lyda's expression it had fallen flat.

"I never offer to do things unless I'm sure," Lyda deadpanned. "Which is something we may need to work on with you, but for now, let's just focus on getting through the day, okay?"

"Okay," Grace agreed, an immense sense of relief washing over her. "But I'm going to owe you one. Or maybe two or three by the time the day is over!"

Lyda snorted. "There is never a shortage of things that need to be done at my shop, but you need to be careful about those offers," she reminded Grace. "The last thing you need right now is another project you don't have time for."

It was hard to admit, but Lyda was right. Grace didn't have time, and it was wrong to make promises she couldn't keep. She would just have to pay Lyda for her time and hope that was enough—something she better talk to Emilio about while she made lunch.

"Thanks, Lyda," Grace called out as she hurried toward the kitchen. "You truly are a lifesaver!"

***

Grace was in the kitchen taste-testing her stew when Lyda and Derek walked in.

"What's up?" Grace asked hesitantly. She wanted to believe her relationship with Derek had improved, especially since he'd spent Christmas at her house the day before, but it was difficult to believe he was at the hotel for a social visit.

In an effort to hide her discomfort, Grace served them each a bowl of the stew and then waited to see their reactions.

"I think it needs a few more minutes," Lyda said around a mouthful of chewy beef.

Derek nodded. "It's good, but a little more salt wouldn't hurt either."

Grace turned back to the stove, added more salt, then covered the pot with a lid and turned back to them. "To what do I owe the pleasure of seeing you again so soon?" she asked Derek.

He held up his hands in mock surrender. "I come in peace, I swear!"

Lyda snorted and rolled her eyes. "That's what they all say."

Derek gave Lyda the side-eye, then turned back to Grace. "Seriously, I just came to see if there's anything I need to know regarding the town's involvement in your newest—" he swept his arm around the room—"whatever this is."

That made sense, especially when she considered how opposed Derek had been to her Christmas plans. Grace picked up a knife and went back to chopping vegetables for the large salad she was making to go with the stew. "I'm sure this will come as a huge disappointment, but I have no plans that will involve the town at this time. And I'm hopeful it will stay that way. I am not supposed to be on the hook for entertainment this time, but these days, it wouldn't surprise me to discover that has changed without my knowledge."

Her words sounded bitter, but Grace couldn't help it. She was stressed out, overwhelmed, and ready to go home and hide, but she couldn't do that. And even if she could, there was a mess waiting for her there too.

The little bell jingled once more and Lyda excused herself. "I better go get that," she said to no one in particular.

Derek cleared his throat. "Well, if things change, please let me know at your earliest convenience. Allen isn't due back until after the first of the year, so I'm still in charge for at least another week."

Grace nodded absentmindedly, then remembered her manners and looked up and smiled. "Thank you," she said sincerely. "I'm sorry I'm being such a grump, I swear it isn't directed at you. If things change—and I really hope they don't—you will be the first person I inform."

"Okay, great," he nodded. "Well, that's all I needed, so..."

DING

They both turned toward the sound, Grace quickly dropping her knife on the counter as she rushed to the oven to pull out the trays of dinner rolls she'd made for lunch. When she turned back, Derek was gone.

"He could have at least said goodbye," she grumbled. "Oh well."

"Are you talking to me or yourself?" Lyda asked as she came back in the room.

"Myself," Grace said with a laugh. "Everything going okay out there?"

Lyda washed her hands, put on a pair of gloves, then began to sort the rolls into baskets. "I'm pretty sure everyone has checked in." She gave Grace a cryptic look. "They're a lively bunch—you're going to have your hands full."

Grace was almost afraid to ask what that meant. "You're scaring me," she joked. "Should I be concerned?"

"Maybe," Lyda replied. She paused to look at Grace, the look on her face softening when she saw the panic return to Grace's face. "I'm sure it's going to be fine," she said quickly. "It's just some of them were a little snappy, but that could have been from traveling."

"I don't believe you," Grace replied, narrowing her eyes. "You wouldn't be warning me over a couple of snappy guests. What's really going on?"

She shrugged, then turned back to the rolls. "It's just a feeling. I can't really explain it." Lyda glanced up at Grace, then back down again. "Please ignore me. I think my personal feelings may be clouding my judgment."

"Do you want to talk about it?" Grace offered, her concern growing at Lyda's cagey responses.

"Perhaps someday," Lyda said dismissively. "Right now, we need to focus on getting lunch ready for the huge crowd of hungry guests you're about to feed."

Grace nodded and turned her attention back to her stew. It was finally ready to serve, so she grabbed a couple of serving bowls and began to fill them. Once that was done, she took the large bowls of stew and salad out to the buffet. Guests were already trickling down, so she shoved all thoughts of Lyda and her guests' potential unruliness aside and focused on getting everyone fed. If she were lucky, it would all sort itself out without her. But when was the last time she was lucky?

Six-Evening

L unch had come and gone, but Grace was still in the kitchen chopping, dicing, slicing, and any other verb you want to throw in there. Her curly red hair was piled high on her head, loose strands sticking out every which way, flour streaked her cheeks, and she could no longer tell what color her apron was supposed to be. Simply put, she was exhausted, but she still had a few more hours to go before she could go home.

Her guests had not been thrilled by her simple lunch plan of stew and salad, and they had no problem letting her know. The next time Grace saw Rebekah, she was going to read her the riot act for promising these people a Michelin star experience when Grace was barely above average as a home cook. She supposed she should have paid better attention to the details when Rebekah had first proposed her plan to have the guests stay at the hotel, but in her defense, it had never crossed her mind people with these kinds of expectations would want to come to Winterwood of all places. Shouldn't they be having their party at some fancy ballroom in some fancy city? And just how were they going to entertain themselves over the next few days?

Grace was going to be absolutely livid if she discovered she was responsible for that.

Grace was just about to pull the last tray of tarts out of the oven when Rebekah walked in, a familiar-looking couple in tow.

"Hi Grace," Rebekah said brightly. "I'd like to introduce you to Alexander and Audrey Bellamy. They're the ones celebrating their anniversary on New Year's!"

Oh great, they were one of the ones who complained about the food. Visions of their previous encounter flashed through her mind:

"Good afternoon," Grace said, smiling at the couple standing before her. "Would you like some stew?" She held up the ladle, showcasing the yummy stew she'd spent hours making.

The woman turned her nose up at Grace's offer. "I assume this is just the starter?" she sniffed. "What's on the menu for the main course?"

Grace gulped as she did her best to hide her surprise. No one had ever complained about the food she'd served before—well, except for that incident during the Mother's Day Experience, but that didn't count.

"Um, actually, I thought a light lunch of soup or salad would be preferable after traveling all morning," Grace stammered.

The man rolled his eyes and turned to the woman. "I warned you about staying in a place like this."

"Yes, and I suppose I should have listened to you," the woman grumbled. *"But the event planner came highly recommended."*

"I suppose we'll have to make the best of it," he replied dryly. *"It will give us a chance to see how the other half live."*

Grace had been tempted to fling the ladle of stew at him, but she'd managed to restrain herself. After the day she'd had, she wasn't sure she could guarantee that level of restraint a second time.

"We've already met," Audrey said, her tone implying a less-than-impressed sentiment.

Rebekah coughed, then smiled at Grace, her right eye twitching a few times. "The Bellamys have expressed concern over the menu," Rebekah explained. "While I have assured them their anniversary party is being catered by one of the best chefs in Kansas City, they—"

"—don't think my homemade food is good enough?" Grace finished for her.

"Um, well, yes," Rebekah said apologetically.

Grace nodded as she wiped another layer of flour off her cheek. "Honestly, I'm not sure what to tell you," Grace told the couple. "You are more than welcome to patronize the other restaurants in town, but I highly doubt you will be any happier with their offerings than you are with mine. So, the way I see it, you have two options: either accept the food I have busted my rear end to prepare for you, or travel to the city and find a restaurant you'll be happy with." Grace turned her attention back to her tarts. "Makes no difference to me, but driving back and forth to the city three times a day holds little appeal in my humble opinion."

"Hrrmph," Audrey said as she stamped her foot in anger. "Never in my life has the help spoken to me in such a disrespectful way."

"Not to your face, anyway," Grace mumbled.

Rebekah sucked in a breath, then quickly grabbed a tart and handed it to Audrey. "She doesn't mean that," Rebekah said quickly. "Please give Grace another chance. She really is a fantastic chef, and well, she's right, there really aren't any other options. Not practical ones anyway."

To Grace's surprise, Audrey accepted the tart and took a tentative bite. It was so quiet in the kitchen, you could have heard a pin drop as everyone held their breath waiting for Audrey's reaction.

"I suppose this isn't the worst thing I've ever eaten," Audrey said after a moment.

Grace held back a smile. Her tarts were the best thing she'd ever made, and few could resist them.

"However," Audrey continued, "I expect more than just soup and salad for dinner. A lot more." She set her partially eaten tart on the counter, then turned on her heel and stalked out of the kitchen, her husband hot on her heels.

When she was sure they were gone, Grace turned to Rebekah and gave her a look, her eyes wide, her brows lifted high.

"I know, I know," Rebekah said apologetically. "I swear she wasn't like that on the phone, or I never would have agreed to work with her."

"I'm not sure I believe you given how often you've exclaimed this party could put your business on the map," Grace replied. "But I will give you the benefit of the doubt." Grace shook her head as she took inventory of the ingredients she'd use to cook the night's meal. "The budget you gave me does not include three-course meals," Grace informed Rebekah. "Nor does it cover the time it's going to take me to cook them."

Rebekah nodded quickly. "I can get you more money," she hurried to agree. "I'll do anything if you'll just promise not to quit on me."

"Of course I'm not going to quit," Grace sighed, though she was sorely tempted. "I'm just not sure how I'm going to do it all alone, that's all."

"What's on the menu for tonight?" Rebekah asked.

Grace looked around for a moment before replying. "I'm almost afraid to tell you," she joked. "But, I've prepared stuffed mushrooms and caprese skewers for the first course, shrimp risotto for the main course, and, obviously, my famous tarts for dessert. Will that meet their approval?"

"It sounds yummy to me!" Rebekah replied enthusiastically.

"What sounds yummy?"

Rebekah and Grace swiveled toward the door where Tom Haverford, Rebekah's 'fiancé,' stood.

"Are you going to follow me everywhere I go?" Rebekah asked angrily. "Because this feels like stalking, and I'm sick of it."

"I wouldn't have to 'stalk' you if you would stop ignoring me and just listen for once," he replied.

Grace gave Tom a hard look. "Wow, those are some controlling boyfriend vibes over there. I can't decide if I should call the police or shame you on socials, but your entitlement is insane."

Rebekah's head turned sharply toward Grace. "He's not my boyfriend," she said curtly. "And you don't even have a social media account."

"He doesn't know that," Grace snarked back. "Honestly, try to help someone…"

Tom, who had been leaning nonchalantly against the door with his arms crossed, straightened up at the mention of socials. "Look," he said, holding up his hands in surrender, "I'm not any happier about all of this than you are, but there are things you don't know. Things that might change your mind, or at the very least, help you understand."

"What kind of things?" Rebekah asked, her eyes narrowed in suspicion. "If this is just another ploy…"

"Your dad is dying," Tom blurted out.

Grace and Rebekah gasped, their hands flying to their mouths in unison.

"That's not possible," Rebekah replied, her head shaking as she tried to process the news. "They would have told me. Someone would have told me!"

"I'm really sorry. Someone should have told you, but you know how your parents are…" Tom trailed off. When he saw how badly shaken Rebekah was, he quickly crossed the room and guided her to one of the stools. "Can you get her some water?" Tom asked Grace.

It took Grace a moment to snap out of the daze she was in, but once she did, she hurried over to the pantry, grabbed a bottle of water, then rushed it back to Rebekah. "Do you want me to call Thorne?" she asked her friend.

Rebekah shook her head. "I need to find my mom. I can't believe she would hide this from me!" She looked up at Tom. "How long have they known?"

"I'm not privy to all the details, but I believe your dad was diagnosed around a year ago. He was supposed to have more time but, well, things have pretty much gone downhill since," Tom replied.

Grace studied Tom as he spoke. He seemed genuine in his responses, but she was having a hard time understanding his place in all this. Why was he so involved with Rebekah's family? Was he an opportunist?

"No, I'm not an opportunist," Tom informed Grace.

A small gasp escaped Grace's lips. "Oh my gosh, did I say that out loud?"

"Yes, you did," Tom said as he rolled his eyes. "The Haverfords and the Rutherfords have been friends for decades. When my father passed away a decade ago, Harvey, who, as you know, is Rebekah's father, took an interest in me. I became his protégé, so to speak."

"If that's the case, then why do you need to marry Rebekah?" Grace asked, genuinely curious. "This seems kind of, I don't know, archaic?"

Rebekah snorted. "Because all these people care about is wealth and status," she said dryly. "I wouldn't be surprised if one of the stipulations of you marrying me is that you have to take the Rutherford name," she said to Tom, her brow raised in question.

Tom gave a curt nod.

"And you're okay with that?" Grace asked incredulously. "I mean, seriously, wouldn't it be easier to just build your own company at this point? Then you can keep your name and marry whomever you want."

A look of doubt briefly crossed Tom's face before he shook it off. "That was the old plan, back when Hunter Parrish was still in the picture. Now that he's gone and I've been chosen as his replacement..." He took a deep breath. "Opportunities like this are once in a lifetime. You simply don't walk away from them."

This was a world Grace would never understand. But did that give her the right to judge these people? If things had been different and she'd grown up a Rutherford instead of a Parker—and she could have, if her family hadn't lost their wealth during the Great Depression—then maybe all of this would seem normal.

Ding

Grace rushed over to the stove to check on the risotto. She really needed to get back on task if she had any hope of having dinner ready on time. Audrey Bellamy was unlikely to tolerate tardiness.

When she turned back, Rebekah and Tom were gone. "What's with everyone leaving without saying goodbye?" she wondered aloud.

***

It was after eleven by the time Grace finally got home. She was so tired, 'exhausted' no longer applied, as she had entered whatever state came after that a couple of hours ago.

Dinner had gone surprisingly well. The guests had raved over her risotto, which had been nice, but after that had come the requests for breakfast. At this point, Grace supposed she should be thankful no one had insisted on two symmetrical boiled eggs and toast cut into four squares with the crust removed. Although, with her luck, someone was bound to be that fussy; it was just a matter of time.

Grace was about to trudge up the stairs when she remembered the mess left over from breakfast. With a groan, she dragged her weary body into the kitchen, only to discover the place was spotless. Had Jilly come back and cleaned after all? Of course she had—who else would have done it?

Since she no longer needed to clean, Grace checked on Granny, saw she was sleeping peacefully, then once again made her way to the stairs. When she reached the top landing, she saw the light was still on under Rebekah's door and decided to check on her, too. She rapped on the door twice, then popped her head in.

"Are you doing okay?" Grace asked Rebekah. She was sprawled out on her bed, still fully dressed, and looked like she'd been crying.

"I'm okay," she replied softly. She sat up and then blew her nose with a tissue. "Mom refused to speak with me. We're supposed to have breakfast in the morning, but it has to be in a public place." Rebekah rolled her eyes. "Mom thinks I won't make a scene if we're in public."

Grace let out an involuntary laugh. "No offense, but I highly doubt that would stop your mother."

"Nope," Rebekah agreed. "And it won't stop me either." She sighed and laid back down. "I was never close to my father, but I still had a right to know," she said sadly.

"I agree," Grace replied. She sat down on the bed beside Rebekah and smoothed her hair out of her face. "I'm sorry there won't be any last-minute reconciliations, but I want to remind you there are plenty of people who love you, without conditions. I know it's not the same, but hopefully that will take some of the sting out of all this."

Rebekah rolled over and hugged Grace. "That means more to me than you'll ever know."

They hugged until Rebekah fell asleep. Once she was sure she wouldn't wake her up, Grace carefully slid off the bed, pulled a blanket over Rebekah, then turned off the light and crept out of the room. Back in her own room, she collapsed on the bed and closed her eyes. One day down, too many more to go.

Five-Morning

To her surprise, Grace woke up before her alarm. She was still exhausted, but she was full of a certain type of hyped-up energy—almost like she'd drank an entire pot of coffee in one sitting, or maybe a case of energy drinks. Regardless, there was nothing to do but hop out of bed and make the most of it.

Since Molly was still holed up next door with Eliza, Grace shoved a pre-made breakfast casserole into the oven, then left Rebekah a note with detailed instructions before leaving for the day. Someone would need to feed the breakfast group, and the only one left to do it was Rebekah. Grace would have to remember to send her a quick text in a little bit, just in case Rebekah skipped the kitchen and headed straight out the door. The last thing Grace needed was to burn breakfast; she already felt terrible enough as it was, leaving the house a mess the day before.

Once she was in her car, she attempted to steer it straight to the hotel, but the car had other ideas. There really wasn't time to stop by the farm, but the little Corolla refused to go anywhere but there. Or maybe it was Grace who just couldn't bring herself to go another day without seeing Cole. Somehow, she'd managed to time it just right and pulled up just as Cole was exiting the house. For a moment, she sat in the warm car and studied the man she was soon to marry. He was dressed in his usual jeans and boots, black Carhartt jacket, and black cowboy hat. Thick leather gloves covered hands that were wrapped tightly around a thermos full of hot coffee. Was it her imagination, or were butterflies dancing in her stomach?

Maybe it was cliché, but her heart still skipped a beat each time she saw him, while her lips automatically turned upward into a large grin. Was this how everyone felt when they were in love? She certainly hoped so; otherwise, what was the point?

When Cole spotted her and turned toward her car, she hurried out and into his waiting arms, throwing hers around his neck and pulling him in for a kiss.

"Good morning to you, too," Cole chuckled against her lips. "To what do I owe this lovely surprise?"

"I missed you," Grace replied, kissing him again. She then leaned her forehead against his, content to be in his arms, even if only for a minute.

Cole leaned back and studied her. "You look tired," he said gently. "Is everything okay?"

Grace sighed, wrapped her arms around his waist beneath his coat, then laid her head against his chest. It was cold, and she dearly wished they could forget everything and spend the day inside in front of the fireplace.

"Everything is fine," she eventually replied. "Just more of the same. My guests hate me, there isn't enough time to get everything done, Jilly is quitting, and I have no one to replace her. You know, the usual."

"Hmm," he murmured against the top of her head. He kissed her red curls and held her tighter. "I know you've had some problematic guests before, but I don't recall that being the norm. Jilly quitting is unfortunate, though. I know now isn't the best time for this, but you should probably consider looking for a replacement."

She nodded and snuggled closer to him, then leaned back and kissed him. "You're right," she said once they parted, "but that will have to wait until after the wedding. I simply don't have time to deal with that right now." Grace checked her watch and grimaced. "I better go. Breakfast ain't gonna cook itself!"

Cole laughed and gave her one last kiss. "Thank you for stopping by, it brightened my day."

"Mine, too," Grace replied, her smile growing. "Any chance I'll see you tonight?"

"Name the time and place and I'll be there."

"I'll text you later," Grace promised. She gave him a small wave, then headed to her car. Coming here had been the right decision, even if she was now running behind. A few minutes alone with Cole, and she was ready to face the most demanding of customers; now she just had to hope this temporary high would get her through the morning.

***

The hotel was eerily silent when Grace entered through the employee entrance in the back. Was everyone still asleep? Had they all left in the middle of the night? No, that was ridiculous—the entire parking lot had been full when she pulled in.

Still, it was disconcerting to be in a place this packed and not hear a single noise. *Oh well*, Grace thought. *Might as well count my blessings.* She entered the kitchen, popped her earbuds in, turned on her "peppy" playlist, and set to work pulling ingredients out of the pantry and fridge while singing along to her favorite song, "Total Eclipse of the Heart." Grace was so engrossed in her task that when she turned around and saw two men watching her from the stools at the counter, she screamed and dropped the pans she was holding, causing a ruckus so loud she was sure she woke the dead—not to mention all the guests in the hotel.

"Sorry about that," one of the men said as he left the stool to help pick up the pans. "We didn't mean to startle you."

"We were trying to do the opposite," the other man assured her. "We thought waiting to get your attention would be less surprising than interrupting. Although," he said sheepishly, "I will say we were enjoying the concert!"

Grace blushed, her face turning the same shade of red as her hair, her heart pounding in her chest as she struggled to get her nerves back in check. "It's okay," she finally got out, her voice thankfully nowhere near as shaky as she feared it would be. "Is there something I can do for you? Breakfast won't be ready for another hour, but if you're hungry now, I have some pastries and coffee I can serve to tide you over?"

The men exchanged a glance, the one returning to his seat at the counter.

"I wouldn't mind some coffee and pastries," the one who helped with the pans replied.

He looked to the other man, who shrugged. "That's not why we're here, but I've never been one to turn down a good cup of coffee."

As Grace poured them each a cup, she struggled to recall where she'd seen them last. She was certain they had been at lunch, and likely dinner, the day before, but couldn't remember their names to save her life. Had they even been introduced? She couldn't recall. That was normally something that would have happened during check-in, but since Lyda had been in charge of that, Grace had missed out on the first meet-and-greet.

When she handed them the cups, the first man stuck out his hand.

"I'm Vincent Cabot, and this over here is my brother Mitchell. We're Audrey's brothers," Vincent explained.

Grace did her best to hide her surprise. These two seemed nothing at all like the snooty woman Grace had interacted with the day before. But maybe she was being unfair to the woman. It was possible that Audrey had simply been having a bad day. Time would tell on that one, but it was uncharitable to judge her harshly based on a couple of unpleasant encounters.

"It's nice to meet you both," Grace replied, remembering her manners. She shook his hand, then turned to Mitchell and shook his as well. "If you aren't here for breakfast, is there something else I can do for you?" She hoped that didn't sound pushy or rude, but she really needed to get back to preparing breakfast before the rest of the guests came down.

The brothers exchanged glances again, then Vincent glanced around the room before leaning forward, his elbows on the counter. "It's like this," he began. "Mitch and I are a couple of bachelors, but we were thinking it might be nice to have a date for the big anniversary party…" He trailed off as he looked at Grace expectantly.

Were they asking her to play matchmaker? She wasn't sure and didn't want to offend them if that wasn't their intent. So how should she respond?

Mitchell cleared his throat. "What my brother is trying to say," he said, as if sensing Grace's confusion, "is that we were hoping you might know a couple of old gals who would like to trip the light fantastic with us old codgers?"

So they were asking her to play matchmaker. The only two women who came to mind were Gladys and Granny, but Grace was pretty sure they were at least a decade older than these men. However, it was only one date, and it would be good for the two women to go out and have fun with people in their age bracket…

"Um, well, I do know a couple of women, but I'll need to talk to them before I make any promises," Grace informed them.

Their faces lit up like little boys on Christmas morning.

"That's great!" Vincent exclaimed. "Just make sure you let them know we'll be perfect gentlemen."

Mitchell nodded. "And if they'd like to go out on a little get-to-know-you date first, we are open to that as well."

"We can even do it here, at the hotel, if that would make them more comfortable," Vincent offered.

Grace smiled at their enthusiasm. This would be good for Granny and Gladys—she could feel it.

"Why don't you let me get breakfast going, and then I'll go talk to the ladies in question?"

Vincent gave a salute, then picked up his coffee and pastry. "Sounds good, we look forward to hearing from you later!"

Mitchell grabbed his coffee and followed Vincent out of the room, the two of them chattering about their upcoming dates.

It was hard not to get caught up in their enthusiasm, but Grace had breakfast for fifty to make and the clock was ticking. So, she put her earbuds in and went back to work. As she said before, this breakfast ain't gonna make itself.

***

Grace was just putting the last breakfast quiche on the buffet when the guests began to file into the dining room. To her somewhat paranoid eye, they actually seemed happy and relaxed, which was in stark contrast to when she'd first seen them at lunch the day before. Maybe they really had just been tired from traveling. She knew some people lived within driving distance, but more than half had come from the airport, so it was possible—likely, even—the journey had been long and stressful. Not that she'd know anything about that. Grace rarely left Winterwood, never mind the state of Missouri.

"Good morning!" Grace said brightly when Audrey and Alexander approached the serving table. "Any plans for the day?" She held her breath as she waited for their reply. She still hadn't been informed if she was responsible for providing entertainment and was concerned she was about to find out in the worst way possible.

"We're going to the theater," Audrey sniffed as she examined the food Grace had prepared. "As I'm sure you know, we will not be here for lunch." She turned to her husband. "One can only hope the theater has standards more in line with ours."

It took all her strength not to slap the serving spoon out of Audrey's hand, but somehow Grace refrained. Honestly, it was a relief to see the older woman fill her plate, even if Grace had to grit her teeth and endure insults as Audrey did so.

Once the couple had returned to their seats, Grace exhaled the breath she hadn't realized she'd been holding—only to inhale sharply once more when she saw Rebekah, Tom, and Jackie enter the dining room. What on earth were they doing here? Surely Rebekah would not allow her mother to make a scene in front of her clients?

The trio made their way to the buffet, grabbed plates, and then proceeded to pick their way through the food.

"I'll have a caramel macchiato," Jackie said to Grace without looking up. "Light. Ice." she said, enunciating each word.

"Best I can do is regular coffee with a flavored creamer," Grace replied, her tone just as dry. "But if you ask nicely, I suppose I could put it in a cup over ice."

Jackie turned her attention to Rebekah. "This is the town you're choosing over your family? You can't even get a decent coffee here." She gave the breakfast table a disdainful look. "Or breakfast, for that matter."

"All the more reason for you to go back home," Rebekah retorted. "But not until after we've had a chance to talk." She turned to Grace and mouthed I'm sorry before leading her mother to a table in the corner.

Would it be wrong to eavesdrop? Is it still considered eavesdropping if Grace just happened to be close enough to overhear? She didn't think so. After all, it wasn't her fault if they talked loud enough she could hear them while she cleaned up the tables around them. Right?

Grace quickly retrieved her cart full of cleaning supplies from the kitchen, then slowly meandered toward the empty tables on that side of the room—tables that absolutely needed to be cleaned that very instant. Audrey would definitely not approve of Grace slacking on the job...

"Why didn't you tell me Dad is dying?" Rebekah asked in a loud whisper. She furiously cut her quiche into tiny pieces, her knife and fork making grating noises against the ceramic plate.

Jackie reached over and stilled Rebekah's hands. "This is not how we behave in public," she admonished. "I didn't tell you because you didn't need to know. You are the one who chose to leave the family, remember?"

"What I remember," Rebekah ground out, "was you disowning me when I refused to come home last May and continue to be your puppet."

"Really, Rebekah," Jackie said, her eyes rolling skyward, "this dramatic side of yours is hardly becoming of a woman of your stature. If you're not careful, you're going to scare Tom off."

Grace angled herself to get a better look at Tom and saw that he looked more amused than offended. She would have to give him credit for that, even if she did think the whole arranged marriage thing was weird and archaic.

"No offense," Rebekah said to Tom, "but I don't care. What I do care about is the fact you're willing to allow Dad to die without even telling me. I'm his only daughter—doesn't he want to see me before..." She trailed off, then sat back in her chair, a defeated look on her face. "He really doesn't, does he?" she whispered.

The atmosphere shifted as a brief look of compassion passed Jackie's face. "You know how your father is," she said dismissively, her hard shell firmly back in place. "If you want to come home, you know what you need to do."

"That's just it," Rebekah said sadly. "I don't want to come home. Not if this is the price I have to pay." She stood up, her chair screeching against the hard granite floor. "I think we've said everything there is to say. I'm sorry, Tom, but I'm officially done being a bartering chip for my parents." She gave one last pleading look to her mom, then rushed out of the dining room, tears streaking down her face.

Grace wanted to rush after her, but Tom beat her to it.

"I bet you're loving every minute of this little 'show,'" Jackie said dryly.

"Are you talking to me?" Grace asked innocently. "Because it breaks my heart to see the way you're treating your daughter."

Jackie placed her napkin over her half-eaten quiche and stood. "If you're so heartbroken over my daughter, do the right thing and encourage her to go home. It's where she belongs. We both know that, even if one of us is too selfish to admit it." She pushed past Grace and left the way she'd come.

Grace watched her go, her emotions warring in her brain. Was she selfish not to encourage Rebekah to go home? While it was true a huge part of her wanted Rebekah to stay, that was not her only motivation. Rebekah deserved to live a life that made her happy, and as far as Grace could see, that did not involve going home to live the life her parents had mapped out for her. No, she would support her friend in whatever decision *she* made. Everyone else was out of luck.

Five-Afternoon

The breakfast dishes were finally done, meat was marinating in the fridge, and dough was proofing on the counter. Did that mean it was time for a break? Grace checked her watch: no, it meant it was time to clean while her guests were at the theater. Oh well, she sighed. They'd been there for less than a day, how dirty could things be? Images of fifty plus people all sharing four bathrooms crossed Grace's mind and she winced; very dirty. Things were likely to be very, very dirty.

When Grace entered the lobby, she encountered Jilly and Audrey in what looked to be a heated conversation. As soon as Audrey spotted Grace, she stopped mid-sentence and waved her over.

"Oh good, I was just informing the maid that we would like fresh sheets, clean towels, and a couple of extra blankets delivered before we get back." Audrey turned her nose up. "And please do something about that bathroom. One of the toilets is clogged and the others stink!"

That was news to Grace, but not unexpected. "I'll make sure it's taken care of," she assured Audrey.

As Audrey moved to put on her coat, an ornate silver locket was exposed around her neck.

"Wow, that's a beautiful necklace!" Grace exclaimed. "It looks antique!"

Jilly turned her attention to Audrey's neck and echoed Grace's sentiment. "It's beautiful," she agreed. Her expression was troubled, but she did her best to smile.

"Thank you," Audrey replied, her hand automatically reaching up to finger the piece. "It's been in my family for generations."

Alexander entered the lobby and proffered his arm, which Audrey immediately took. They were a handsome couple, dressed in matching floor-length black wool coats, black leather gloves, and white cashmere scarves. Alexander was dressed in a suit, while Audrey wore a long, velvet black gown that Grace would have sworn was an evening gown, which was strange. They looked like they were dressed for a night at the opera, not the small theater and restaurant in the city. But what did Grace know? That was one more place she'd never been, despite sending her guests there at least once. She really did need to get out more.

"I hope you have a lovely time," Grace called out after them.

Audrey waved over her shoulder, but did not turn back.

"She is really something," Jilly said once they were out of earshot.

"You have no idea," Grace replied. She filled Jilly in on all the things she'd missed while they gathered the cleaning supplies and headed toward the bathrooms. "Want to split up?" She faced the women's bathroom and did her best to steel herself for what was to come. Someday, she was going to let Molly have this experience. It might make her think twice about booking these large gatherings. Although, to be fair, Grace had agreed to this one.

"I think it might be faster if we tackle them together," Jilly replied absentmindedly.

Grace studied her for a moment before pushing the cleaning cart through the door and grabbing the glass cleaner and rags. She decided to start with something easy and work her way up to the grosser parts of the job.

"Before I forget," Grace said as she sprayed the mirrors positioned over the sinks. "Thanks for going back to the house yesterday and cleaning up. It was a huge relief to go home to a clean kitchen after spending all day here."

Jilly's head snapped toward Grace. "Are you being sarcastic?" she asked suspiciously. "I told you I would go back if I could, I'm sorry I wasn't able to, but it just seems mean to try to make me feel bad about it."

"What are you talking about?" Grace asked, her face a mask of bewilderment. "I'm not trying to make you feel bad. The kitchen really was clean when I got home, so I just assumed..." She trailed off as she tried to think of who else could be the mysterious cleaning fairy. "If it wasn't you, then who?"

They stared at each other for a moment before Jilly broke down in tears.

"I'm so sorry, I was out of line. I'm just so stressed out I automatically thought the worst and went on the attack."

She sighed as she wiped her nose with the sleeve of her sweater. "Please forgive me."

Grace grabbed a couple of tissues from the box on the counter, handed them to Jilly, then gave her a hug. "There's nothing to forgive," she said quietly. "Is there anything I can do? At the very least I can listen."

"I hate to burden you with my problems," Jilly replied.

"A little drama might make the job go by faster," Grace joked. When Jilly didn't smile, Grace's grin faltered. "Seriously, it might help to talk to someone. If you don't want it to be me, that's fine, but all this stress isn't good for you."

Jilly nodded, then turned back to the mirror. "You're right, it's just hard." She took a deep breath, then let it out slowly. "Bea and I have finalized the paperwork, which is exciting, but also terrifying. I am officially the owner of Bea's Bakery."

"That's great news!" Grace replied. A grin spread across her face as she looked at Jilly in the mirror. "So what's wrong?"

"The same thing that's always wrong," Jilly sighed, "money. I know Bea has been profitable, so I'm not too worried, but a lot of her customers have been with her for decades. What if they no longer wish to support a new baker? I've invested almost everything I have in this business venture; I can't afford to fail."

"I can't see that happening," Grace assured her. "This town has a way of supporting each other. Plus, you're the only bakery within a thirty-minute drive. I see no reason why people would suddenly decide to make that drive every time they need a cookie!"

A tiny smile tugged at Jilly's lips. "You're probably right." She let out a breath, her shoulders relaxing a bit. "Thanks, Grace."

"Anytime," Grace replied. She stepped back to admire their handiwork. The mirrors looked good as new, all the toothpaste splatter, hairspray mist, and water spots now gone. "Ready to tackle the toilets?"

Jilly wrinkled her nose and looked over her shoulder at the stalls. "No, but we might as well get it over with."

Grace approached the first stall, saw the mountain of toilet paper stuffed inside the bowl, and groaned. "I don't get paid enough for this," she joked.

"You could always come work for me at the bakery," Jilly offered, her brow raised in hope.

"You have no idea how tempting of an offer that is!"

***

Grace only had one hour of freedom before she needed to head back to the hotel to get dinner ready, and she decided to use that hour to talk to Granny and Gladys about Vincent and Mitchell. She was still convinced this would be a good thing for them; however, she was concerned about them doing too much and worsening their health problems. Both struggled with mobility issues on "bad days," but lately, there had been fewer of those. Still...

She parked the car on the side of the street facing the sun and hurried inside. To her surprise, the first thing she noticed was the kitchen: it was clean for the second day in a row. Grace knew she hadn't done it, Jilly had been with her all afternoon, Rebekah was out at the winery, and Molly was still holed up next door. So, who could it have been?

"Alright gals," Grace said as she entered Granny's room. "Who's the mysterious person doing all the cleaning around here?"

They looked up from the rerun of *I Love Lucy* they were watching and stared at Grace.

"We did it," Gladys replied. She shrugged and turned back to the television.

While Grace stood there and stared in disbelief, they laughed at one of Lucy's antics, completely oblivious to the turmoil Grace was experiencing.

"We're not helpless, you know," Granny said, patting Grace on the arm.

"That's right," Gladys nodded. "We can handle a few dishes from time to time."

As the one who usually did the kitchen cleanup, Grace knew there were far more than "a few." Especially on the days when they had guests, like yesterday.

"Thank you," Grace finally replied. She did her best to shake off her surprise before she offended them. "Um, I have something to talk to you two about if you have a minute?"

Granny switched off the television and turned to give Grace her full attention, Gladys following suit. "Of course, dear, what can we do for you?"

Why did she suddenly feel so nervous? In order to buy some time, Grace pulled up a chair, sat down, then cleared her throat. "As you know, there's a big anniversary party in a few days out at the winery..." Grace began, her nerves causing her hands to sweat. She wiped them on her jeans and cleared her throat a second time.

"Spit it out, dear, us old gals don't have time for these theatrics," Gladys teased.

"A couple of gentlemen are looking for dates and I volunteered you," Grace said, her words coming out in a rush.

Gladys and Granny exchanged amused glances.

"In my day, if a gentleman wanted a date, he asked the lady himself," Granny replied. She hid her smile behind a handkerchief as she watched Grace squirm.

"Um, well, yes, but in their defense, I told them I needed to talk to you first before I gave them the opportunity." She pulled at the collar of her sweater and fanned her face. This should not be as awkward as she was making it. "They also offered to have coffee, or even dinner with you before the party if that would make you more comfortable?"

Granny glanced at Gladys once more before taking pity on Grace. "We would be happy to accompany the gentlemen," she informed her. "I can't remember the last time I went out on the town with a gentleman caller!"

"I haven't been out since my husband passed, and that was almost two decades ago!" Gladys exclaimed.

Grace watched their animated expressions and felt a deep sense of loss and regret for them. If it had been twenty years for Gladys, it had likely been closer to thirty for

Granny. It was hard not to feel responsible. Granny had dedicated her life to caring for Grace. She had put her own wants and needs on hold, and now that Grace was an adult, Granny had health problems that kept her out of the dating game. At some point in the future, Grace would make it her mission to help Granny find a boyfriend. It was the least she could do after all Granny had done for her. Gladys, too. Grace had no doubt the two of them would love to double date. This experience with the brothers could be a trial run.

"I will let them know when I see them tonight at dinner!" Grace slapped her knees then stood. "Speaking of which, I better get back to the hotel. Do you prefer a coffee or dinner date?"

"I'm leaning toward lunch," Gladys replied. "What about you, Josie, do you agree?"

Granny nodded. "I think that would be a good compromise. Lunch doesn't hold the same degree of formality as dinner, yet is a little more formal than a cup of coffee."

Grace wasn't sure what that meant, but she didn't have time to figure it out, so if they were happy, she would be happy too. "I'll make the arrangements." She gave them each a hug on her way out, then headed back to her car. A sense of relief washed over her as soon as she was back outside. Things were actually going well. If you forget about all the minor complaints, which she was most definitely going to do!

Five-Evening

Grace stared at her third attempt at a Beef Wellington and briefly wondered if she'd maxed out her capabilities as a fine dining chef with the previous night's risotto. The wellington had looked so simple on the cooking video, yet for some reason, her bottoms were always soggy, and the inside was drier than the Sahara. As the seconds on the clock ticked down, her panic began to tick up. She obviously couldn't serve this mess, so what could she do? There wasn't time to find another recipe, and besides that, there was no other meat defrosted.

"Everything okay in here?" Jilly called from the doorway.

The sound of an unexpected voice caused Grace to jump, the knife she'd just used to cut open the meat pie/pastry/roll—whatever it was supposed to be—falling from her hand and clattering against the granite floor.

"Sorry," Jilly said apologetically. "I didn't mean to scare you, I just wanted to make sure you didn't need any help before I left for the day."

"I thought you'd already left," Grace replied as she leaned over to grab the knife.

She walked over to the sink and rinsed the utensil before placing it in the dishwasher, then spun around and gave Jilly a pleading look. "Help me!"

Jilly laughed as she entered the kitchen and placed her coat and purse on the counter. "What's wrong?"

Grace waved her hand over her failed dish as if she were a model on *The Price is Right* displaying a prize. "As you can see, I've ruined dinner. I have a little over an hour before the guests expect to be served and nothing to serve them. Please tell me there's some magic you can work to fix this?"

"This is for the same guests that expect Julia Child-level food from a small hotel chef in the middle of nowhere?" When Grace nodded, Jilly walked over to the food and examined it, sighed, and then cocked her head as if an idea had suddenly come to mind. "It's possible we could turn this into a Steak Diane. Given the current state of this sad, sad piece of meat, I think smothering it in a sauce is our only option."

"I've never heard of that, but I'm desperate enough to try anything," Grace replied eagerly. "What would I serve with it?"

Jilly thought about it. "Considering the time constraints, and the number of diners, I would go with mashed potatoes, sautéed green beans, and a crusty French bread if you have it."

Grace nodded as she mentally checked the inventory she had left. "I can make that work. Thanks, Jilly, you're a lifesaver!"

"I'm always happy to help!" Her smile faded as she rolled up the sleeves of her sweater and set to work cutting the beef tenderloin into slices.

While Jilly worked on that, Grace began pulling ingredients out of the pantry. She was just about to start on the mashed potatoes when Vincent and Mitchell walked in.

"Something smells good!" Vincent said, his nose in the air as he sniffed. He beamed at Grace, completely oblivious to the catastrophe he'd almost walked in on. "Did you have a chance to talk to those two lovely ladies?"

"I did," Grace replied, returning his smile. "And I'm happy to report they have accepted your invitation!"

Vincent and Mitchell high-fived.

"That is great news! Do they want to get together for coffee tomorrow?" Mitchell asked.

Grace shook her head. "Actually, they preferred lunch. Does that work for you? They could come here to the hotel, or there's a diner in town if you want a little privacy." Grace thought about that for a moment. "Well, I shouldn't say privacy—the place is likely to be packed with locals—I just mean—"

"—privacy from the prying eyes of our family members?" Vincent finished for her. He laughed at the embarrassed look on her face. "We all know my sister can be...intense," he said with another laugh, "the last thing we want to do is scare the ladies off before the big night!"

Granny and Gladys were made of sterner stuff than that, but Grace was reluctant to ask them to face the scrutiny of Audrey Bellamy if they didn't have to. This was a big deal for them, their first 'date' in decades. She wanted them to have fun, not spend their time in the crosshairs of Audrey's disapproving gaze. On the other hand, if they went to Addie's, Vincent and Mitchell were likely to end up on the wrong end of a few of those gazes themselves. But Grace had a feeling they would revel in their newfound celebrity status, so Addie's it was.

"I'll give you directions tomorrow morning," she told them. "I need to get these potatoes on, or dinner will be late!"

"If there's one thing my sister hates, it's tardiness," Vincent replied.

Mitchell nodded his head in agreement. "She fired our maid for being two minutes late once, and Audrey was only eight at the time."

Grace gasped. "Your parents allowed her to do that?"

"Oh yes," Vincent said, his face expressionless. "If they had curtailed her reign of terror instead of encouraged it, she might not be the person she is today." Vincent shrugged. "But what do you do? Audrey is family, so if she says jump, we ask how high."

Having grown up an only child, Grace was quick to admit she had no knowledge or experience with sibling dynamics. However, it was difficult for her to understand why grown adults in their seventies and eighties would continue to allow themselves to be dictated to by their sister. Unless... could she be funding their lifestyle? Grace shook her head; this was neither her business nor her problem. Besides, it was probably some rich-person thing she was unlikely to ever understand.

Instead of responding, she gave an awkward chuckle, then excused herself to see to those mashed potatoes. If she were lucky—and she rarely was—dinner would go off without a hitch, and she just might make it out of there in time to see Cole.

***

On her way out the door, Grace texted Cole she'd meet him at the farm as soon as she finished checking on Granny. It wouldn't be much of a romantic date, but sometimes snuggling in front of the fireplace was enough. Most times, actually. Oh, who was she kidding—it was enough every single time. All she needed was him; even the fireplace was optional.

Back at the house, she found Granny and Gladys in Granny's room watching a documentary on cold cases.

"Should you two be watching that this close to bedtime?" Grace asked. She did her best to hide her smile at the twin looks of indignation she received, but she failed. "I'm just teasing," she laughed.

"You're probably not wrong," Gladys admitted sheepishly. "It's just hard to look away."

"We're becoming armchair detectives!" Granny said enthusiastically.

Grace smiled at their enthusiasm. At this point, she would happily indulge any whim that kept her Granny active and interested in life. Memories of last Christmas, and almost losing her, still haunted Grace from time to time.

"I'll order some of those murder mystery games for you to solve," Grace volunteered. "In the meantime, I have an update on your dates!"

Gladys switched off the television as they both gave Grace their full attention.

"You'll be meeting Vincent and Mitchell at Addie's tomorrow at noon!"

Granny turned toward Gladys, her eyes wide in horror. "What are we going to wear?"

"Forget about that, look at my hair! It's been ages since I've had it cut and dyed."

They turned to Grace.

"What are we going to do?" they cried in unison.

Grace's eyes grew big as she tried to process this sudden change in demeanor. She had expected excitement, not whatever this was. An idea popped into her head.

"I know what you need—makeovers!" she exclaimed. "I'll make the arrangements for tomorrow morning, before your lunch date, okay?"

They turned toward each other again and appeared to communicate without words before turning back to Grace and nodding.

"That should be fine, dear," Granny nodded. "It will make for a long day, but I think we can handle that."

"I'm sure a nap will be in order when we get home, but that's no different than any other day!" Gladys said cheerfully.

"Great! Then it's settled! I will pick you two up after I finish breakfast at the hotel, and we'll go from there." Grace gave them a stern look. "You may go back to your show now, but do try not to get too engrossed. You don't want to have nightmares."

Gladys snorted. "I'm staying over tonight, so we can watch as many scary shows as we want, Mom!"

Grace raised her brow. "Did Molly kick you out?" Surely she hadn't gone crazy enough to kick Gladys out of her own home over a cold.

"I kicked myself out," Gladys replied. "I love that woman, but you'd think that poor baby had the plague with the way Molly is carrying on. It's her first child, so I'll give her some grace, but I need to do it from here for sanity's sake."

"I don't blame you," Grace replied. "I offered to drop off some food yesterday, and she banned me from the house entirely. Said she didn't want any germs I might have picked up from the guests to infiltrate through the plates. At that point, I wished her well and told her to call me when it's safe again."

Gladys nodded. "That was wise. Now all we can do is hope she comes to her senses. If she decides to fear germs from now on...well, we might need to do an intervention."

"Let's hope it doesn't come to that," Grace agreed. She checked her watch. "If you two have everything you need, I'm going to head back out?"

Granny patted Grace's hand. "We're fine here, dear girl. Go have some fun with that handsome young man of yours. Lord knows you could use a break!"

Grace bent down and hugged Granny, then reached over to give Gladys a quick hug as well. "Make sure you call me if you need me, okay?"

They nodded in unison, then Gladys picked up the remote and turned the television back on. Within seconds, they were glued to the screen again, which left Grace feeling confident it was safe to leave them on their own for a few hours.

After another quick text to Cole letting him know she was on her way, she locked up the house, hopped back in her car, then headed to the farm. The closer she got to Cole, the faster her stress seemed to melt away. She was almost free of it completely by the time she was standing in the doorway, her arms wrapped around his neck as he held her close.

Once inside, she laughed as Ruby and Max tackled her to the floor and licked her face. "I missed you, too," she said, petting them both on the head. After a few more minutes of pets, they grew bored and returned to their beds in front of the fireplace. "They're getting lazy," Grace teased Cole.

He shrugged. "That'll change once spring comes along. Then you'll be hard-pressed to get them inside."

Grace smiled as he helped her off the floor. "They aren't the only ones who've missed you," he said, leading her over to the couch.

As soon as she sat down and kicked off her shoes, she noticed the spread on the coffee table. All her favorite fruits, cheeses, and chocolates were laid out, rose petals scattered between them. Soft jazz music sounded through the speakers as Cole handed her a champagne flute full of sparkling grape juice. Her stomach rumbled as her eyes filled with tears at the thoughtful gesture.

"Thank you," she whispered as she kissed his cheek.

"I figured you could use a little pampering." He grinned. "When was the last time you ate?" he asked as he handed her a small plate.

When was the last time she'd eaten? She tried to think back through the day, but her memories were mostly of her awkward conversation with Granny and Gladys and the mess she'd made of dinner.

"I'm not sure I did," she finally replied. "I do sample the food as I cook it, though, so I've at least had a few bites here and there."

"Hmm, next time I'll add some protein to your snack board," Cole mused. "For now, we'll have to make do with what we have."

Grace laughed as she admired his handiwork once more. "Yes, this will be such a hardship," she teased. She filled her plate then leaned back against his chest and stretched her legs out on the couch. "Thank you," she said again. "There are no words to describe how much I needed this right now."

Cole wrapped his arm around her and kissed the top of her head. "Rough day?"

"Yes, but I'd rather not waste time talking about it." Piper walked into the room and made a beeline for the couch, hopping up into Grace's lap in one smooth jump. "Hello, sweet girl," Grace cooed to the kitten. "Have you been good for Cole?"

He snorted but reached over to pat Piper on the head. "Let's just say it will be a relief to take down the Christmas tree."

"Want to do it now?" Grace asked, silently praying he said no. She felt terrible that her cat had been terrorizing the tree and knew she needed to do something about it, but she was so tired, and oh so comfortable in his arms, she didn't want to move.

"It can wait," he said, as if sensing her inner thoughts. "For now, I'm happy just to hold you."

Grace leaned back and kissed him, then situated herself against him once more. This time with him had been just what she needed. Tomorrow was a new day, and she was now ready to face it. Well, maybe not just yet.

Four-Morning

When Grace arrived at the hotel, she was greeted by the sight of a police car parked out front. "What on earth?" she said aloud. Concerned for her guests, she rushed inside, fear that someone was ill or hurt gripping her chest in a vise.

The second she opened the door, she was thrust into chaos, the lobby full of people screaming as a panicked-looking Officer Smith attempted to calm them down. Boy, did Grace wish Rebekah was there to do one of her high-pitched, attention-getting whistles. Out of desperation, Grace attempted one, but what came out was closer to the sound of a paper airplane nosediving to the ground than the ear-piercing shriek she was going for.

Since that wasn't going to work, Grace walked over to one of the chairs, stood on top of it, and screamed, "Everyone quiet down!" Once she had their attention, she straightened her spine and summoned every ounce of courage and self-esteem she'd accrued over the last year and commanded them to remain silent until they were asked to speak.

As expected, Audrey did not take kindly to that and forced her way to where Grace was standing. She pointed her finger at Grace and sneered. "I will not remain silent while your thief of a maid goes free." She turned to Officer Smith and stuck her finger in his face. "I want that woman arrested immediately!"

Alexander stepped over to his wife and grabbed the hand she was using to point at Officer Smith. "Now, now, dear, why don't we give the man some space to actually do his job."

"The only job he needs to do is put handcuffs on that woman and cart her thieving behind over to the local jail," she said through gritted teeth. "I have no doubt that a few minutes behind bars will jog her memory and then my locket will mysteriously reappear."

Grace gave a pleading look to Officer Smith. "Can you please tell me what's going on?"

"I received a call this morning that there'd been a theft here at the hotel. When I arrived, this woman"—he gestured toward Audrey—"informed me that Jilly had stolen her locket."

"What?" Grace asked, her eyes widening in shock. "That's not possible. Jilly wouldn't do something like that."

Audrey snorted. "Oh sure," she said sarcastically as she rolled her eyes, "someone like that would *never* steal."

"No, she wouldn't," Grace asserted forcefully. "Was anything else stolen?"

Before Audrey could reply, Officer Smith turned to address Grace. "That's what I was trying to ascertain when all heck broke loose."

Vincent stepped forward and raised his hand. "According to everyone I've spoken to, nothing else appears to be missing."

Officer Smith nodded in thanks. "How about this—I want everyone to return to their rooms and do a thorough search. We'll all meet back here in fifteen minutes; that should be more than enough to check your belongings."

Everyone but Audrey and Alexander trudged back to their rooms.

"That includes you two as well," Officer Smith informed them.

Audrey looked like she was about to refuse, but Alexander took her by the arm and led her away.

Grace watched them go, then carefully climbed down off the chair. "It makes no sense that she would accuse Jilly," Grace mumbled, more to herself than to the officer. "Jilly is not a thief."

"Sometimes desperate people do desperate things," Officer Smith replied.

Jilly had been having a difficult time as of late, and Grace might be willing to agree she was desperate, but that didn't make her a thief. "If that were true, why take the necklace? Why not go for cash, or electronics, or diamonds?" Grace shook her head; the longer she talked, the more absurd this became. "I saw the locket. I'm not an expert, but in my opinion, its value does not extend very far beyond the sentimental."

"Are you saying it's ugly?" Officer Smith asked, a grin spreading across his face.

"Not ugly per se, gaudy is a better word. Perhaps ostentatious. But those things can be valuable, so it's not that," she mused as she tried to put her thoughts into words. "The locket is silver, it's just—these people are rich," she blurted out. "If someone were really willing to sneak into the hotel in the middle of the night and risk getting caught, why not steal as much as they possibly could?"

Officer Smith narrowed his eyes. "How do you know they snuck in in the middle of the night?"

"Because Audrey was wearing the necklace at dinner last night, so it wasn't possible for it to have been stolen before then," Grace said defensively. Was he really accusing her of stealing the necklace? Because that would truly beat all, wouldn't it?

As if sensing where her thoughts were going, Officer Smith was quick to hold up his hands in surrender. "Let's not start down this path again," he implored her. "I'm honestly just trying to do my job. I'm not accusing anyone of any wrongdoing, okay?"

Grace wasn't sure about that, but ultimately decided it would be better for her, and Jilly, to get along with the officer. "Fine," she agreed. "I just don't want to see my friend get falsely accused of something she didn't do. In a town this size, that could ruin her entire reputation, you know?"

He nodded in agreement. "These days, a rumor is all it takes."

One by one, the guests re-entered the lobby, Vincent leading the way. "I've checked with everyone, and no one's missing anything." The rest of them nodded behind him. "If that's all, may we head to breakfast now? This has been a rather taxing way to start our day, and I think some coffee is in order."

Normally, Grace would have agreed. The only problem was, she was the one in charge of making that coffee, and she hadn't had a chance. Now the guests had double the reason to be upset. This was definitely going to lead to some bad reviews.

"I need to go take care of that," Grace whispered in Officer Smith's ear. When he nodded, she hurried to the kitchen and got the coffee going in record time. Since there was no way the guests would wait an hour for her to get a hot meal together, she called Bea over at the bakery and put in an S.O.S. order for whatever donuts and pastries she had on hand. It would likely wipe her out for the day, but Grace doubted Bea would mind going home a little earlier than usual.

Grace was pouring the last cup of coffee when Bea appeared in the dining room, boxes in hand. "Oh, thank God!" Grace exclaimed as she took the boxes and laid them out on the table. "This is not a happy bunch," she whispered to Bea.

"I can see that," Bea whispered back. "And I noticed Officer Smith in the lobby when I came in. What's going on?"

"I'll have to tell you later," Grace said out of the side of her mouth. She pasted a smile on her face and turned to face the crowd. "Please help yourselves," she announced as she gestured toward the table. To her immense relief, once Vincent and Mitchell got up, the rest began to follow. She would have to give them a special thank-you later that day.

Now that was done, Grace grabbed the coffee carafes and headed back to the kitchen to refill them, Bea in tow. "One of the guests is accusing Jilly of stealing a family heirloom," Grace informed Bea once they were out of earshot.

"That's not possible," Bea said firmly. "That child would give you the shirt off her back. No way would she ever take something that didn't belong to her."

"I agree," Grace replied quickly. "But that isn't stopping them from accusing her."

"Why are they accusing her specifically?" Bea asked.

Grace thought back to Audrey's earlier statements. "Because she's a maid," Grace stated. "Apparently in Audrey's world, that's all it takes to make one a criminal."

Bea scrunched up her nose. "That makes absolutely no sense."

"Tell me about it," Grace agreed. "But Audrey is determined, and I have no idea what to do about it."

"Surely Officer Smith will intervene," Bea stated, her tone confident. "You can accuse someone all you want, but without proof, there's not much you can do about it. And around here, being a maid ain't proof."

Although she agreed, Grace wasn't sure there was "nothing" they could do, but she didn't want to borrow trouble by voicing all the ways she was concerned they could hurt Jilly. At this point, all she could do was hope that either the necklace turned up before any permanent damage was done.

Officer Smith cautiously entered the kitchen. "Any chance I could get a cup of coffee?"

Without thought, Grace grabbed a to-go cup and filled it up. She handed it to him, then waited for him to take a sip before bombarding him with questions. "Did the Bellamys finally see reason? Is Jilly in trouble? Is there anything we can do to help her? Is it possible to keep this from getting to the rumor mill?"

"Whoa, Grace, slow down," he replied. He took another sip and then set the cup down on the counter. "They are still adamant Jilly is the thief, but without proof, there isn't much I can do about it. I'll need to bring her in for questioning, but beyond that, unless she confesses, I don't see much coming of this."

"Can you interview her here instead of at the station?" Grace implored. "The last thing she needs is for people to see her go in there and start asking questions."

He nodded thoughtfully. "I still need to interview the rest of the guests, see if anyone saw or heard anything last night. If you can get her down here today, I don't see any reason why we can't do the interview here."

"Thank you so much," Grace replied in relief. "I'll call her now and see what time she's available." She pulled her phone out of her pocket and looked up Jilly's number. "Please help yourself to some of the pastries out on the buffet," Grace told him. "It sounds like it's going to be a multiple-donut kind of day."

"Got any chocolate eclairs?" When Bea nodded, he grinned. "Well, don't mind if I do then. Ladies." He tipped his hat, then exited the room.

"I need to get going, honey, but don't you worry, this will all blow over, okay?" Bea patted Grace's arm, then grabbed her keys.

Grace wanted desperately to believe her, but the pit in her stomach was making that impossible. Why did there have to be problems every single time she agreed to host? Could she really not catch a break? Or was this just what her life was like now?

As she waited for Jilly to answer the phone, Grace checked her watch. Shoot! She was supposed to pick up Granny and Gladys and take them to their first appointments at Lulu's Hair Salon. Plus, she needed to talk to Vincent and Mitchell about their lunch at noon.

A scary thought hit her: would they even be able to leave the hotel for lunch? If Officer Smith required everyone to stay until they'd all been interviewed, that could take all day. She leaned her elbows on the counter and groaned.

"Hi, Grace, what's up?" Jilly said once she answered the phone.

Grace pulled her phone away from her ear and looked at it in surprise. She'd forgotten she'd already dialed the number as she stood there lamenting her newest problem.

As gently as she could, she explained the situation to Jilly and asked her to come to the hotel.

"But I have an alibi," Jilly protested.

"That's great!" Grace said as she perked up. "All you need to do is tell it to Officer Smith and we can put this all behind us." Well, the necklace was still missing, so there was that, but at least the part about Jilly being a thief would be over. Although, without her as a suspect, the Bellamys might turn their suspicions on Grace. Luckily for her, she too had an alibi.

Jilly sighed and made a noise that sounded like a sob. "I'll be there as soon as possible."

It wasn't her fault, but Grace had never felt lower in her entire life. She knew this was the last thing Jilly needed, and resolved to do whatever she could to help.

As Grace waited, she checked in with Vincent and Mitchell.

"How are you guys holding up?" she asked the brothers. She looked around the room and saw Audrey glaring at her from a table in the back.

They looked up at her in surprise.

"We're fine," Vincent replied nonchalantly. "It's Audrey you need to worry about. She's like a dog with a bone and won't be satisfied until someone's head is on a platter."

Of that, Grace had no doubt. But she had no desire to stir the pot with the guys who just last night claimed to be under their sister's thumb. So, she decided to focus on their date instead.

"I fear this might cause a delay with your lunch date..." she said, hopeful they'd get the message.

Mitchell nodded his head. "Might be best to postpone to tomorrow. Even if we can get out of here in time, I fear the stress might make us bad company."

Even though she agreed, Grace found his reply intriguing. Hadn't his brother just said they were fine? It's not like it was their necklace that had gone missing. Maybe they really were closer to Audrey than Grace thought.

"I will let the gals know," Grace informed them. She took the opportunity to run back to the safety of the kitchen and out of sight of Audrey, who was still glaring daggers at Grace.

Back in the kitchen, Grace made a few calls as well as arrangements to get Granny and Gladys to their new appointments. Hopefully, once Jilly's interview was over, she and Grace would be free to leave.

"I got here as fast as I could," Jilly announced as she entered the kitchen through the servants' entrance. She was out of breath, as if she'd literally run there.

Alarmed at the look of pure terror on her face, Grace immediately crossed the kitchen and took Jilly into her arms. "Hey, it's okay," she said, rubbing soothing circles on Jilly's back. "No one really believes you stole the necklace. This is just a formality."

"Audrey believes it," Jilly sobbed.

"She doesn't count," Grace hurried to assure her. "For all we know, this is some sort of insurance scam and you're nothing more than a convenient scapegoat."

Officer Smith chose that moment to enter the kitchen. He stopped in his tracks as soon as he heard Grace's words. "That's an interesting possibility," he mused. After a moment, he shook off his thoughts. "Regardless, I need to follow procedure, so let's get this over with." He motioned for Jilly to take a seat at the counter across from him. "I promise not to bite," he teased. When Jilly didn't smile, he cleared his throat. "Can you tell me where you were last night between the hours of eleven and six this morning?"

Jilly sucked in a breath and squeezed her eyes shut. "Can you promise this won't leave this room?"

"Unfortunately, no," he said apologetically. "Your answer will need to go in my official report, but I can say that most people won't have access to that."

"I was with Derek," she said, her voice barely above a whisper.

Grace gasped and exchanged looks of shock with Officer Smith. "The interim mayor?"

"He's also a real estate agent," Jilly said defensively. "He's been trying to help me find a place for me and my kids. I had to wait until the kids were in bed to meet him." She shook her head in embarrassment. "I was so tired I ended up falling asleep on his couch midway through our search of available houses."

"Will he vouch for you?" Officer Smith asked gently.

"I don't see why he wouldn't." She reached out and clasped Officer Smith's arm in a death grip. "Please," she implored. "I can't give my in-laws anything to use against me. They'll take my kids." Her voice broke, and she lowered her head so they couldn't see the tears in her eyes.

He squeezed her hand, compassion on his face. "I'll do everything I can to keep this under wraps," he promised.

"Thank you," Jilly replied softly. She let go of his arm, pushed her stool back, then turned to Grace. "I hope you don't mind, but I think it's best I pass on performing my maid duties today."

Even though she should have seen that coming a mile away, Grace was still caught off guard. "Of course," she said, when what she really wanted to do was beg Jilly to change her mind. Without her, things would take at least twice as long.

Officer Smith pushed his stool back and nodded toward Grace. "I better get back out there. You're free to do whatever you need to do, but please don't go too far. I may need your help."

What he could possibly need her help with, she wasn't sure she wanted to know, but she smiled and nodded anyway. As it was, now that Jilly was gone, she was likely to be stuck there all day anyway. She really needed to find a replacement for Jilly. Her sanity depended on it.

Four-Afternoon

The guests were supposed to go out for lunch, but due to unforeseen circumstances, they had canceled their plans. That meant Grace was now on the hook for providing lunch. Out of sheer spite, she once again prepared stew with the leftover tenderloin from last night's failed Beef Wellington and a plain garden salad. Okay, spite and a lack of other options. Besides that, she honestly didn't care anymore. After this latest stunt, Grace had zero desire to cater to Audrey's whims.

When she served the admittedly lackluster meal, the look of disgust on Audrey's face was more than enough to make up for the extra work Grace had to perform. Now, all she had to do was tackle all the cleaning, take Granny and Gladys to their appointments, and prepare dinner for fifty. No big deal.

Grace was pushing the cleaning cart through the lobby when the door swung open and Lyda came in, a burst of cold wind following close behind.

"What's going on?" she asked, her eyes lit up in delight. "I heard there's been a theft. Has the thief been caught? Do you know who it is? Do *I* know who it is?"

Despite everything that had happened, Grace laughed at her enthusiasm, then quickly sobered when she realized the impact of Lyda's questions. "Who did you hear that from?"

"So it's true," Lyda exclaimed. "They're talking about it all over town! When I stopped by Addie's this morning, some of the regulars were taking bets on who it could be, though I didn't recognize any of the names."

That was a good sign. Lyda would have definitely recognized Jilly's name if she'd heard it. Hopefully, that meant no one actually knew anything and this was nothing more than town gossip that would go away as soon as a new scandal replaced it.

"I'm not sure what's true," Grace hedged. "All I know is something is missing. Lost, even. There is no proof that a theft has taken place."

Lyda eyed the cleaning cart. "If I help clean will you give me all the dirt, so to speak?"

"If by dirt, you mean the literal dirt I have to vacuum up, sure!"

"You know exactly what I mean," Lyda accused. "Come on, Grace, don't hold out on me."

Grace motioned for Lyda to follow and led her to the first of the downstairs bathrooms. "Honestly, Lyda, I'm surprised by you. I would have never thought a no-nonsense woman like you would be prone to gossip."

She appeared to consider that, then quickly dismissed it. "Maybe I just want to be involved in the goings-on of the town," she offered up as a possible excuse. "Or maybe

I want to make sure I didn't just move my kids to a town crawling with criminals."

If she was serious—and Grace hoped she wasn't—that was concerning. The last thing Winterwood needed was a reputation for being unsafe. Truthfully, it was the last thing Grace needed. No one would want to visit a B&B in a dangerous town.

"I can assure you the town is not teeming with criminals," Grace replied. "A necklace has gone missing, but it couldn't possibly be anything other than an accident. Perhaps it fell behind a nightstand." She stared into the sink she was cleaning. "Or maybe even down a drain."

"You sound awfully convinced," Lyda pointed out. "Why is that?"

"Because the person they've accused couldn't possibly have done it," Grace blurted out.

Lyda stopped cleaning the mirrors and whirled to face Grace. "Aha! I knew there was more going on than you've let on. Come on, tell me who the alleged culprit is!"

Grace knew better than to gossip. Hadn't she learned her lesson last 4th of July? But Lyda was her friend. Surely it wouldn't hurt to tell her. She might even have a solution; she usually did. "Jilly." Grace regretted sharing that the second Jilly's name left her lips. She'd promised she'd help keep this under wraps, then told the first person who'd come along. No, scratch that—the second person who'd come along. Bea had been the first, and like Lyda, Grace had barely hesitated to open her big mouth. "Please don't tell anyone," Grace begged. "If this got out, it could destroy her, and I know for a fact she's innocent."

"And how do you know that?" Lyda asked in a way that implied she already knew the answer.

Had this been nothing more than a fishing expedition? Was Lyda here because she knew about Jilly and Derek and was looking for confirmation? If that were the case, Grace was in big trouble. "She has an alibi," Grace said noncommittally. "Anyway, I need to get this done so I can take Granny and Gladys to their hair appointments. They have a big date coming up!" She waited rather impatiently to see if Lyda would take the bait and allow a change of topic.

"You're telling me that not one, but two women in their eighties managed to find someone to date before I did?" she asked incredulously. "Wow, I feel very lame right now."

The relief Grace felt that Lyda had dropped the Jilly topic was quickly replaced with guilt for hurting her friend. "The dates are with a couple of guys who are staying at the hotel," Grace explained. "It's practically a one-time thing—well, two-time if you count the getting-to-know-you lunch date. But that's all."

"Still," Lyda said, her face a mix of confusion and disbelief. She shook her head and went back to cleaning the mirror. "Whatever. I keep saying I'm fine being single, it's time for me to either commit to that or start actively looking for a man. It's not fair to be upset when one fails to fall out of the sky and land in my lap. Even if"—she gave Grace the side-eye—"that seems to happen for others."

Grace tried to hold back a grin. "I know it's hard to believe, but there are some single men in Winterwood. If you're serious about dating again, I'm sure I could help you out."

"I'll think about it," Lyda shrugged. "For now, let's focus on cleaning so you can get out of here." They cleaned in silence for a few moments before Lyda continued. "Is it always this chaotic around here?" she asked thoughtfully. "I feel like Christmas was a bit chaotic, too."

It was hard to admit, but yeah, she had a point. "Unfortunately, yes, but I'm choosing to believe that's a normal part of owning a hospitality business."

"You're not wrong," Lyda conceded. "I've had my share of difficult customers. I guess I've just been fortunate enough to build my business to a place where I can now afford to tell them to go take a long walk off a short pier, you know what I mean? But it wasn't always like that."

Grace wanted to ask about some of Lyda's earlier experiences. She had a feeling she could learn a lot from the woman, both in business and personal life. However, there simply wasn't time. Not today, anyway.

They hurried through the rest of the chores, and by the time they were done, the bathrooms were spotless, and all the rooms had been vacuumed, along with the hallways and lobby. Grace did not provide daily typical housekeeping services like making beds, changing sheets, or cleaning the rooms. She didn't have the manpower for that, so it was more of an every-other-day kind of thing, depending on the length of the guests' stay—and the number of guests.

"Please send Emilio a text with the number of hours you worked," Grace said to Lyda as they were getting ready to leave. "I want to make sure you're properly paid for all the help you've been giving me."

"You don't have to do that, but I appreciate it," Lyda replied. "Where are you off to first?"

"Lulu's Hair Salon," Grace replied. "Want to come? Granny and Gladys are a hoot to be around. It should be fun!"

Lyda checked her watch. "You know what, I would love to. I still have a couple of hours until the boys get home, might as well make them count!"

"Awesome! If you want, you can leave your car here and ride with me. I just need to run home and pick up the gals real quick, and then we'll be off!"

"Sounds good!"

Grace peeked into the dining room, saw that everyone was still occupied with Officer Smith, then quickly shut the door before she was seen. Time to get out of there while she still could.

"Let's go!" she urged Lyda.

They ran to Grace's car like they were being chased by zombies, laughing like schoolgirls the whole way. Once there, they hopped in and collapsed in their seats, out of breath like they'd just run a marathon.

"We need to do this more often," Grace mused.

"What's 'this'?" Lyda asked. "Run away from the hotel?"

"No," Grace shook her head and smiled. "Have fun."

"I couldn't agree more!"

***

Granny and Gladys were so excited about their trip to the hair salon, they were waiting on the porch when Grace and Lyda pulled up to the front of the house. As happy as Grace was to witness Granny's enthusiasm, a part of her also felt guilty. She'd spent the last year of her life working her rear end off but hadn't thought once to take Granny out or pamper her a little. What good was making money if you didn't treat the ones who made it possible once in a while? From now on, she would make it her mission to see that Granny had at least one fun experience a month—more if she could make it happen.

Grace and Lyda hopped out of the car and hurried to the porch to help the ladies down the steps.

"How long have you been waiting out in the cold?" Grace asked, her voice tinged with concern. The last thing she wanted was for one of them to catch a cold.

"We came out when we saw your car coming up the road," Granny explained. "We were watching through the window."

In all the years Grace had lived with her grandmother, she could not remember a single time she had done that. She must be even more eager than Grace thought.

Once everyone was settled in the car with their seat belts on, Grace drove the one mile across town and pulled up in front of Lulu's. "Do you two have an idea of the kind of haircut you want?" Grace asked, her interest stirred.

For as long as she'd known her, Granny had had long, straight, gray hair she typically wore up in a bun. It would be interesting to see what style she chose now that she had a choice.

"I'm thinking I might like something like Blanche from *Golden Girls*," Gladys replied thoughtfully.

Granny nodded. "That would look good on you," she replied earnestly. "I'm thinking I might like to try a haircut similar to Dorothy's."

"When she wore it a little longer?" Gladys asked.

"Yes!" Granny exclaimed. "What do you think, Grace?"

Grace tried her best to imagine Granny with short hair, but she couldn't do it. "I think if that's what you want, you should go for it!" She exited the car and hurried to help Granny out of the backseat as Lyda did the same with Gladys.

As they moved toward the door, Grace felt a drop of something cold and wet land on the back of her neck. She looked up at the now white sky and sighed. The forecasted snow had finally arrived. So much for her hope it would hold off until after the new year.

"Hey y'all," Lula called out as they entered the brightly lit salon. "Right over here," she said, motioning for Granny and Gladys to sit in the salon chairs. She gave Grace and Lyda a once-over. "You know, we had a couple of cancellations if you two want a turn as well. It could be fun! We can do a big reveal once everyone is done!"

Lyda subconsciously reached up and touched her hair. "I suppose I could do with a trim," she mused. She eyed Grace's messy bun. "What about you, Grace?"

"I don't know," Grace hedged. "My hair is so curly, haircuts have always been a nightmare."

A woman Grace didn't know piped up from her workstation. "I specialize in curly hair," she informed Grace. She motioned for Grace to take her hair down, then spent a few moments studying it. "If you prefer to keep your hair long, I think you'd be happy if we gave it a trim and some long layers. Maybe even some bangs if you're feeling adventurous?"

"You would look so cute in bangs," Granny exclaimed from her seat. "You should do it, honey, it'll be a treat!"

It was hard to argue with Granny's enthusiasm, so Grace reluctantly agreed. "I guess there's plenty of time before the wedding for it to grow out if I don't like it," she mused. She turned to Lyda. "I'm only doing it if you'll do it, too, though."

Lyda nodded and they took their seats in the salon chairs opposite Granny and Gladys.

"As long as I don't end up with Sophia's haircut," Lyda joked.

"Does that make me Rose?" Grace asked, her eyes narrowed.

"You're too nice to be anyone else," Gladys called over her shoulder. "You should consider that a compliment!"

Grace thought back to the reruns she watched with Granny as a kid. "Do you guys remember the time all the ladies went to see Sophia's hairstylist and he gave them all her haircut?"

Lula snorted. "I remember that well, but I promise we won't do that to you!"

"I'd look like a poodle!" Grace exclaimed.

"I'm not sure what I would look like, but I know I don't want to find out!" Lyda chimed in.

Talk turned to New Year's Eve and plans for the big night. "You ladies doing anything special?" Lula asked.

"We have dates!" Granny told her.

Gladys held up her hand. "A couple of gentlemen have invited us out to the winery for their sister's fiftieth wedding anniversary!"

"Fancy!" Lula said as she fluffed Granny's hair. "Don't forget all us little people as you're hobnobbing with the rich and famous! Well, maybe not famous. But I've heard they're rich!"

"Where'd you hear that?" Grace asked, her curiosity piqued. She knew she hadn't said anything to anyone other than Rebekah and Jilly, and she doubted either of them were spreading that news around town.

"Oh, honey, we hear everything here," Lula replied. She waved a hand as if to brush off the thought.

Grace watched the mirror intently as the hairdresser worked. As long as she was able to keep putting her hair up in buns, she wouldn't be too upset, but she was still a little concerned. The last time she'd had bangs was in middle school, and she didn't remember liking them. Then another thought flashed through her mind: what if Cole saw her new hairdo and hated it?

"Relax, Grace," Lyda said, her eyes boring into Grace's through the mirrors. "It's just hair. Even if you hate it, which I doubt given the way it looks so far, it will grow back."

Lyda was right, she did need to relax. She was pretty certain the stress from that morning's unexpected events was getting to her, but if she were honest, she tended to be stressed out a lot these days anyway. Luckily, the noise from the hairdryers prevented Grace from replying, since she was concerned her response may have come out harsher than intended.

A few minutes later, Lula announced they were ready for the big reveal. "On the count of three we're going to spin your chairs around. Are you ladies ready?"

"Yes!" they cried out in unison.

"Okay then—one, two, three!" Lula spun Granny around as the other hairdressers also turned the rest of the chairs.

"Wow!" Grace exclaimed as she saw Granny's new look. "You look amazing!" She turned to see Gladys, her shock growing at how different and sophisticated they looked. "You, too, Gladys!"

They both preened as they happily fawned over each other's new look. Then they turned to face Grace and Lyda.

"Don't you both look lovely!" Gladys said as she examined each of them. "I love the bangs, Grace, they were a good choice. And Lyda, I love the shorter do—not many can pull that off, but it looks great on you!"

Grace turned to look at Lyda and had to agree with Gladys—Lyda looked great! She'd chosen a pixie cut, which Grace would never have the confidence to do, but on Lyda it worked well. "You look like a movie star," Grace gushed.

Lyda rolled her eyes but couldn't keep the grin off her face. "You're too much," she said with a playful flick of her hand.

"Well, I for one think you all look absolutely stunning!" Lula announced. "How about a picture?" She grabbed her cell phone off the counter and motioned for everyone to group together.

"Would you mind taking one for me, too?" Grace asked as she pulled her phone out of her pocket.

"Oh, me too!" Lyda said as she also grabbed her phone.

Lula laughed as she pulled up the camera app. "How about I make this easy on us and text you all the pictures when I'm done?"

That worked for Grace, so she wrapped her arm around Granny's waist and smiled. She couldn't wait to see the pictures—and the huge grin on Granny's face. This would be another memory she would cherish for the rest of her life.

Four-Evening

As tempting as it was to serve soup and salad again for dinner, Grace decided it was not wise to further antagonize Audrey. After all, she was a paying guest. And if the missing necklace wasn't some kind of insurance scheme—which, let's be honest, Grace had no reason to assume it was—then Audrey was a victim. Of what, Grace wasn't sure. Had the necklace really been stolen? Was it misplaced? Had the clasp broken and the necklace was somewhere in the hotel? These were the questions that had plagued her since she'd dropped Gladys and Granny back off at the house. Maybe it was time for a little detective work. Or at least a sweep of the hotel grounds. Did she know anyone who owned a metal detector?

"Something sure smells good in here," Officer Smith said as he entered the kitchen through the dining room. "What's for supper?"

Grace looked up from the pistachios she was smashing. "We're having burrata with candied pistachios, condensed balsamic, extra virgin olive oil, salt, pepper, chopped fresh herbs, and crostinis for the appetizer. Spinach ravioli in a truffle butter sauce for the entrée. And lemon mousse for dessert."

His eyes got bigger with each item listed. "I don't know what you just said, but dang, I had no idea you were such a fancy cook!"

She pointed toward the tablet she'd propped up on the counter next to her. "I'm not, I'm just decent at following instructions. If you'd been here last night, you'd have borne witness to one of my spectacular failures. The only reason I survived was Jilly...speaking of which..."

Officer Smith chuckled. "I see what you did there," he said, his appreciation for her cleverness evident. "There's not much to tell on that front. I spoke with the interim mayor and he confirmed Jilly's whereabouts. No one here claimed to see or hear anything last night, though there were a few who I feel know more than they're sharing. At this point, there's not much I can do about that either, other than file an official report and contact the local pawn shops in case the necklace happens to find its way to one of those."

"You really think that will happen?" Grace asked, her brows raised in surprise. When he shrugged, she shook her head. "I'm honestly just having such a hard time believing it was stolen. Or, if it was, that someone did it for money." She leaned forward on the counter and spoke so no one would overhear. "You saw those people," she whispered. "They aren't exactly hurting for money."

"Looks can be deceiving," he said cryptically. "When I asked if Mrs. Bellamy had proof of the value of the necklace, she rolled her eyes and said it was worth more than my entire salary for the year." He blew out a breath, his eyes flashing. "When I reiterated that I needed proof, she became angry, said it was a family heirloom, and how dare I imply her family valuables were anything other than, well, valuable."

After spending a couple of days getting to know Audrey, Grace had no problem picturing the exchange in her head. "She's—something else."

"You're not kidding," Officer Smith agreed. "Anyway, I think I'm finally done here. If you happen to come across anything suspicious, please give me a call."

Grace quickly grabbed a to-go box and filled it with items from that night's menu. She then handed it to Officer Smith. "You earned this," she joked.

He sniffed the container and let out a contented sigh. "Thanks, Grace. You have no idea how much I'm looking forward to going home and enjoying this."

She was pretty sure she did know, as she too was also looking forward to going home. Unfortunately for her, she still had many hours to go until she could. With a sigh, she waved goodbye, then returned to crushing the nuts.

"Well, how nice of you to spend the day pampering yourself instead of working," Audrey sneered as she entered the kitchen.

Startled, Grace dropped the rolling pin and sent the nuts flying in every direction. "You almost gave me a heart attack," she gasped, her hand flying to her chest. She took a couple of deep breaths as she tried to calm her racing heart. "Is there something you need? Dinner should be ready in half an hour."

"We're famished," Audrey huffed. "If you had been here like you were supposed to be, you could have provided drinks and snacks while we sat through that dreadful interrogation that inept officer 'conducted.' It's honestly the least you could have done."

Grace wanted to protest, to defend herself against this newest accusation, but Audrey was right; she should have done that. It was especially remiss of her not to do so on a day like today, when the guests had no other recourse. She had been so excited to take Granny out, it had just never crossed her mind the guests might have needed her here.

"I'm so sorry," Grace began, painfully aware that an apology would not cut it. "The appetizers are almost ready. If you can give me five more minutes, I promise to have them out to you."

"Hmmph," she sniffed. "See that you do." She turned to exit the kitchen the way she'd come. "And, Grace," she called over her shoulder. "Unless you want this to be the last party you and your little friend ever host, I suggest you worry more about your guests and less about your hair."

Grace reached up and touched her curls. It just figured the one time she decided to do something for herself, someone decided to use it as ammunition against her.

An immense sense of guilt set in as she assembled the burrata platters. Audrey had included Rebekah in her threat, despite Rebekah having nothing to do with any of this. The last thing Grace wanted was to harm Rebekah's career and reputation, but that was exactly what she was doing.

On the other hand, was she supposed to have let Granny down? Grace sighed for the umpteenth time that day. Is this what it was like being a parent? Always having to choose between kids, husband, work, etc.? No, she was just being dramatic. She'd never had back-to-back guests to care for before and was just struggling to adjust to the new demands on her time.

She put the final drizzle of olive oil on the platters and then stepped back to admire her handiwork; they looked amazing, if she did say so herself. Now, all she had to do was hope that Audrey agreed.

"What on earth is going on over here?" Rebekah demanded as she entered the kitchen. There was a light dusting of snow on her coat and hair, the powdery white in stark contrast to her red cheeks. "I've been receiving texts from Audrey all day," Rebekah said as she held up her phone. "She's threatening to cancel the party!"

"Hold that thought," Grace said as she picked up a couple of the platters and backed out of the swinging doors to the dining room. She repeated the process until all of the platters had been relocated and dispersed to the hungry guests. "Okay," Grace said as she wiped her brow. "I can talk, but I need to get this pasta plated as I do so."

Rebekah plopped down on a nearby stool. "Fine," she huffed. "I don't care what you do, as long as you explain why I'm about to lose the biggest client of my career."

Her tone of voice was accusatory, but Grace did her best not to take offense. It was obvious her friend was distressed, and Grace couldn't help but wonder if there was more going on than a difficult client. "So, basically, a family heirloom has gone missing, and I failed to provide refreshments throughout the afternoon while the guests hung around to give statements to the police."

"That's it?" Rebekah asked, her eyes rapidly blinking as she tried to digest that information. "I mean, fine, that's not great, but Audrey made it sound like there was a sale at Nordstrom's and you took the last pair of boots in her size."

The room went silent, the only sound coming from the stove as steam hissed out of a boiling pot of pasta. It started with a grin Grace couldn't contain that quickly morphed into a giggle. Then, she made the fatal mistake of looking at Rebekah. Once she saw her narrowed eyes and raised brow, the giggle turned into a guffaw, and before she knew it, Grace was on the floor laughing so hard there were tears running down her face.

"I have no idea what you think is so funny," Rebekah huffed. She did her best to maintain her haughty demeanor, but eventually caved and joined Grace on the floor in laughter. "I suppose it might be a little funny," she gasped as she wiped her eyes.

They sat there a few minutes longer as they tried to catch their breath, then Rebekah reached over and turned Grace's face toward hers.

"The bangs suit you," she said, giving her official stamp of approval. "I should have recommended them a long time ago." She went quiet for a moment. "Is that why you weren't here this afternoon? Because you were out getting a haircut?"

"I took Granny and Gladys out for a little makeover before their dates with Vincent and Mitchell," Grace said defensively. "I was already there when Lula said there was a cancellation and offered me the spot."

Rebekah put her arm around Grace's shoulders and pulled her close. "I'm sorry, I didn't mean to bite your head off earlier. And I'm not accusing you of anything now. I'm just trying to figure out the best way to smooth things over with Audrey, and to do that, I need to know what happened."

Grace hugged Rebekah back, then stood, washed her hands, and began plating again. She had no idea how to fix things, but she knew cold food wasn't the answer. "She accused Jilly of stealing her locket. That's what started this whole mess," Grace informed her.

"Wow, I did not see that coming!"

"Me neither," Grace replied. She winced as she realized, once again, how easy it was for her to open her big mouth and gossip. The only thing that made her feel even a little bit better was that Rebekah genuinely needed to know. "Jilly had an alibi," Grace added quickly.

Rebekah held up her hand. "You don't need to defend her to me. I know she would never do something like that." She reclaimed her seat at the counter and stared at Grace for a moment. "Any idea what really happened to the necklace?"

Grace shook her head. "I've spent all day trying to figure that out. The best I can come up with is that it fell behind a piece of furniture or the clasp broke and it's lying around the grounds somewhere. I've been thinking about borrowing a metal detector and doing a quick sweep to see if I can find it."

"Let me know when you do it and I'll come and help," Rebekah volunteered. "Right now, I better get out there and talk to the Bellamys." She inspected the plates of pasta then looked back at Grace. "Any chance you can spare another one of these?" she said, indicating the plates. "I haven't eaten all day."

"Of course," Grace replied. She shooed Rebekah out of the kitchen and hurried to finish the main course. No one had yet complained about still being hungry, but she preferred to keep it that way.

Once dinner had been served, Grace worked on putting the finishing touches on the lemon mousse. She was relieved she'd picked an easy dessert, especially given how difficult it was to serve fifty on her own. She really needed some help. But was it possible to hire someone to help for such a short amount of time? Maybe Lyda would agree if she asked nicely. It seemed wrong to beg when her friend was currently on vacation from her own job, but desperate times and all that.

With that settled, Grace grabbed her cart, pushed it into the dining room, and began to clear the dinner plates, just in time to see Tom Haverford walk in. She abandoned her cart and rushed to meet him before he could locate Rebekah in the crowd.

"I realize this is technically a place of business, but it is currently closed to the public," she whispered fiercely.

Tom's perpetual amused expression remained firmly in place. "Relax, Grace, I was invited."

"By whom?" she asked incredulously. Surely Rebekah would have mentioned something like that.

"By Audrey Bellamy," he informed her. "She and Alexander are good friends of my parents, and when they heard I was in town, they invited me for dinner."

That was rude, but believable. Leave it to Audrey to add dinner guests without informing the one person who needed to know: the chef. Luckily for all of them, Grace always prepared extra.

"In that case," she said through gritted teeth, "allow me to show you to your table." She led him to the back corner where Audrey had claimed "her table." "If you will give me one moment," she said once Tom was seated, "I will prepare your meal."

"Make sure you're quick about it," Audrey said tersely. "I've seen faster service from a rout of snails."

Rebekah squirmed uncomfortably in her seat before rising and excusing herself. "I better help Grace," she called over her shoulder as she practically ran for her life. "What's he doing here?" she whispered once they were back in the kitchen.

"Audrey invited him," Grace whispered back. "Why? I thought you two were getting along these days?"

"If by getting along you mean he's been doing his best to charm me into an arranged marriage, then sure, we're the best of buds," she said dryly.

Grace shrugged helplessly. "There's not much I can do. The Queen of Mean is allowed to invite guests to dinner if she wants to. Now, if you'll excuse me, I better hurry before she decides to start whacking me with a shoe!"

Once the plate had been prepared, Rebekah held out her hand and motioned for Grace to hand it to her. "I'll take it," she said, her tone brooking no argument. "It's the least I can do to make up for the nightmare I've put you through."

"It's not your fault, but I appreciate it anyway," Grace said softly. "I still need to finish clearing the dinnerware before I serve dessert, and this will help."

"Plus, it will keep you from facing the Ice Queen," Rebekah joked.

They walked toward the dining room together and through the doors.

"You know, it wasn't that long ago I nicknamed you that!" Grace teased.

"I have no doubt I earned it every bit as much as Audrey has, possibly more so," Rebekah replied. She gave Grace a mock salute and then marched to the table like a soldier facing a firing squad.

Grace watched her go, concern eating at her. There were only four more days to go—could they survive them?

Three-Morning

The light snow the day before had turned heavy overnight, and by the time Grace woke up there were at least a couple of inches covering the ground, as well as the road. Since she didn't live on one of the main streets, it would be hours before a plow arrived. Which was plenty of time for the roads to be cleared before Granny's big lunch date, but zero time before she needed to get to the hotel.

Since there was no way her little Corolla would make it out of the driveway, that left one option: to trudge through the snow on foot. In the dark. In the cold. While everyone else was snuggled up in their warm beds. But she wasn't bitter about that—no, not at all...

Grace put on as many sweaters as she could layer on top of each other, pulled on her snow boots, hat, and gloves, then squeezed into her winter coat. She felt like the kid from *A Christmas Story* but figured it was better than frostbite. At least it was too dark out for anyone to see her.

Before she left, she pulled another casserole out of the freezer and placed it in the preheated oven for the breakfast gang. She wasn't sure who was even showing up these days, but at the very least Granny and Gladys would need to eat. With that done, she started the coffee maker, then made her way to the front door.

Her hand on the knob, Grace took a deep breath, let it out slowly, then quickly opened the door and braced for the wave of cold. Surprisingly, it wasn't that bad. Refreshing, even, but that could be because she hadn't stepped foot outside the house yet. She decided to ride the wave of positivity and practically launched herself outside, careful not to slip on the snow-covered porch.

As she made her way down the stairs, her hands wrapped around the railing in a death grip, she was briefly illuminated in the headlights of an oncoming vehicle. She winced, hoping the driver was too busy navigating the slick roads to notice her, then winced again when they pulled over in front of the house. Seconds later, a pair of black boots descended onto the white expanse, and she watched with interest as the rest of the man was revealed once he stepped out from behind the truck door.

"Cole!" she squealed, momentarily forgetting her less-than-appealing appearance. She waddled over to him as fast as she could, then tried to wrap her arms around his neck, only to find them too restricted by her layers to reach him. Her cheeks reddened from embarrassment. Or was it the cold? No, it was definitely embarrassment.

He took pity on her and leaned down to kiss her, just barely managing to hide his amusement. "Do I want to know why you're dressed like that?" he asked, his head cocked to the side as he looked her up and down.

"I need to get to the hotel and I didn't want to freeze," she stated matter-of-factly. "By the way, what are you doing here? Not that I'm not happy to see you," she added quickly. "I've just never seen you off the farm so early in the morning."

Cole took her gloved hand in his and helped her over to the passenger side of the truck. "I see you missed my text this morning," he drawled. "I told you I would come by and pick you up since I knew you wouldn't be able to drive on your own."

Grace looked back at him, as best she could, and grinned. "You really are the best fiancé in the world, aren't you?"

"I'm just trying to keep up with how amazing you are," he replied. He kissed her nose, then turned his attention to getting her up into the truck, his smile fading as he realized just how tall of an ask that was. "Any chance we can remove some of your clothing?"

Her eyes went wide. "Cole!" she gasped. "In the middle of the street? How scandalous!"

"This town is due for a little scandal," he quipped. "Now, seriously, I don't think we're getting you in otherwise."

The warmth of the truck was calling to her, so she allowed him to help her out of the coat, as well as several layers of sweaters. Once she was left with only two, her arms were able to move freely again and she climbed up into the cab. Cole handed her the discarded clothing, then went around to the other side and climbed in.

They drove to the hotel in silence. The trip, which usually took less than three minutes, took at least twice that. When they arrived, he hurried back to her side and helped her out of the truck and onto the sidewalk.

"Do you have any ice melt?" he asked as he surveyed the area. "You don't want anyone to slip and fall should they decide to go out in this weather."

"I think we have some in the little storage shed in the back," she replied. It was one more thing to add to her to-do list, but better that than get sued. "I'll take care of it as soon as I get breakfast in the oven."

Cole was already on his way back to the truck when he called out over his shoulder, "Don't worry about it, it should only take me a few minutes."

Before she could protest, he'd hopped back into the cab and was pulling out onto the street—presumably to go get the ice melt out of the shed. She would have to find a way to thank him later, but for now, the least she could do was get coffee on so he had a warm drink to look forward to.

In stark contrast to the day before, the hotel lobby was blissfully silent when Grace entered. It was almost spooky as she crossed the granite floors, the only light coming from the two windows. She turned on the lamps, bathing the room in a soft yellow glow, then screamed and jumped at least a foot when a figure appeared in the doorway.

"Sorry," Vincent said, holding up his hands in surrender. "I didn't mean to scare you, although"—he began to chuckle—"your reaction was probably one of the funniest things I've seen in quite a while."

Grace did not smile in return, nor did she join in his laughter. She could feel her heart racing as she struggled to calm her breathing. Boy, would she be glad when her life returned to normal. Who knows how many years that little episode just took off her life!

"Is there something I can do for you?" she asked once she'd found her voice.

Vincent shook his head. "I couldn't sleep, so I thought I'd see if there was any coffee. No worries, though, I can wait until it's breakfast time."

"I was just about to put some on," Grace replied, her hostess side kicking into full gear. If she was going to get back in her guests' good graces, going above and beyond was a good first step. "If you want, you can come with me, or I can bring you a cup as soon as it's done?"

"If it's all the same to you, I might as well tag along," he said, falling into step beside her. He leaned toward her and lowered his voice. "Mitch snores," he said conspiratorially. "He'll never admit it, but it's driving me crazy!"

She could only imagine how challenging it would be to share a room with someone like that, her mind wandering back to Mother's Day when Rebekah complained about the same thing regarding Hunter's mom, Amelia. That conversation had led to the thawing of their frosty relationship. So maybe a little snoring wasn't the end of the world after all.

"I can see if I can move you to a separate room," Grace offered. They'd reached the kitchen, and she busied herself filling the large commercial coffee machines with coffee grinds. More than once she'd wished she had one of these back at the house. Maybe next time she hosted there she could borrow one...

Vincent pulled out a stool and made himself comfortable. "Nah," he eventually said, "it's tempting, but it would hurt Mitch's feelings. No sense in creating drama over a few days of lost sleep."

Grace was relieved to hear him say that. While she felt offering up another room was the right thing to do, it would have created more work for her, and she was already drowning in the work she had. "How do you feel about a tomato, onion, and goat cheese frittata for breakfast?"

"Sounds amazing to me," Vincent shrugged. "But I don't think I'm the one you're trying to impress...."

He wasn't wrong, but Grace still wanted the rest of her guests to enjoy their stay as well. "I've heard the kids are coming tomorrow," she said as a way to change the topic. When he began to laugh, Grace gave him a quizzical look. "What's so funny?"

"I've just always found it amusing to hear adults in their fifties referred to as 'the kids,'" he explained. "But I don't have children, so I'm probably not a good judge of these things."

Once again, he wasn't wrong—it was a little strange. She'd had her share of being called "the kid," but what else did you refer to someone's kids as?

As she was chopping the tomatoes and onions, Cole came in through the back door.

"I cleared as much of the sidewalk as I could and laid down the ice melt," he said, kissing the top of her head. "I would still discourage the guests from leaving until the roads have been cleared, but they should at least be safe walking from the hotel to their cars."

Grace reached up and kissed his cheek, then stopped chopping long enough to pour him a fresh cup of coffee. "I owe you big time!"

"Who's this?" Vincent asked, his brows drawn in confusion. Or was it concern?

Cole walked over and held out his hand. "I'm Grace's fiancé, Cole," he explained. "I assume you're one of the guests staying here?"

"Yes," Vincent replied.

He shook Cole's hand but chose not to introduce himself, something Grace found curious. Cole was the kind of man most people instantly liked and respected, so it was weird to see someone appear to do neither—if the look on Vincent's face was any indication.

"I better leave you to it," Vincent said as he pushed back the stool and stood. "Looking forward to breakfast," he called over his shoulder on the way out.

Once he was gone, Grace turned to Cole, her expression one of confusion and concern. "What do you think that was all about?"

"No clue," Cole shrugged. "I'd love to stay and chat, but I need to get back to the farm. Call me when you're ready to leave and I'll come pick you up."

While it was a sweet offer, and would definitely earn him a bunch of brownie points, there was no way she was bothering him again—especially so soon after his heroic rescue this morning.

She wrapped her arms around him and pulled him close, then leaned up and kissed him goodbye. "I'll call you later."

With a quick tip of his cowboy hat, he was gone, leaving her alone with the breakfast crowd. It was time to call Lyda and beg for help. All she could do now was pray and hope Lyda said yes.

Three-Afternoon

B reakfast had gone as well as could be expected. Audrey didn't exactly do cartwheels around the dining room while exclaiming she'd just eaten the best frittata of her life, but she didn't complain either, so Grace considered that a win. When Grace had finally mustered up the nerve to call Lyda, she'd graciously agreed to help. Her kids were spending the week with their grandparents, and she claimed to be bored out of her mind. When Grace told her she felt guilty asking her to work on her vacation, Lyda assured her she was doing her a favor. Someday soon Grace would have to find a way to return the favor. But all of that could wait. For now, she just wanted to focus on Granny and getting her ready for her date!

By now, most of the roads in town had been cleared. Lyda had come in to help with breakfast clean-up, and once she'd heard about the trip to Chrissy's Boutique for new outfits for Granny and Gladys, she'd volunteered to chauffeur for that too. So, Grace sent Cole a quick text informing him of the new plan and then set out for home to pick up the ladies.

When they pulled up in front of the house, Lyda surveyed the snow-covered steps and walkway. "Do you think the two of them will be able to navigate the snow?" she asked, a look of doubt crossing her face.

Grace sighed and zipped up her coat. "Give me ten minutes," she said as she hopped out of the car. *There truly was always something, wasn't there?* she muttered to herself as she hurried around back to the garage where they stored the lawn equipment. Three minutes later, she was back out front shoveling the steps and walkway, Granny and Gladys waiting patiently in the foyer. When she was done, she propped the shovel up on the side of the porch and then helped the gals down to Lyda's waiting car.

Once they were all seated again, Grace turned in the passenger seat to face Granny and Gladys in the back. "Are you excited for your dates?"

"At our age, we're excited to get out of bed in the morning and not break a hip!" Gladys joked.

Grace winced at the reminder of Gladys doing exactly that almost a year ago.

"C'mon, Grace, lighten up," Gladys chastised. "And yes, we are both excited!" She jostled Granny with her elbow, and both of them giggled.

They pulled up to the curb in front of Chrissy's and carefully exited the car. Grace rushed ahead and held the door open as the other three shuffled in.

"Good morning!" Chrissy said brightly. She ushered Granny and Gladys over to a plush loveseat she had positioned in the back of the room, then handed them each a glass of sparkling cider. "So, tell me what you're looking for?"

Granny and Gladys exchanged wide-eyed glances.

"We weren't expecting the royal treatment!" Granny exclaimed. "Do you do this for all of your customers?"

"Just the special ones," Chrissy replied, her smile never leaving her face. She handed Grace and Lyda glasses as well, then resumed her position, an expectant look on her face.

Gladys and Granny exchanged looks again.

"Well, we don't know," Gladys said, her earlier enthusiasm waning a bit. "What do women these days wear to a lunch date?"

"Hmm," Chrissy murmured as she studied them. "Since it's freezing out there, how about fleece-lined leggings, a long-sleeved blouse, and a sweater?" Without waiting for a reply, she walked around the store, pulled items off the racks, and draped them over her arm. Once she was done, she returned to the dressing area and began to assemble the items on nearby mannequins. "What do you think?" she asked once she was done. "I think you two would look very smart in these outfits."

Grace could not have agreed more and began to seriously consider coming back for a makeover of her own.

"I love it!" Granny gushed. She folded her hands together and held them under her chin as she grinned.

"Me too!" Gladys exclaimed, her movements mimicking Granny's. "Can we try them on? You know, just in case."

"Of course," Chrissy assured them. "Give me a second and I'll set up a couple of dressing rooms."

Grace and Lyda waited patiently for Chrissy to finish, then they waited patiently some more for Granny and Gladys to change. When they finally exited the dressing rooms, Grace and Lyda clapped with approval.

"You look amazing!" Grace said enthusiastically as she leapt up from the couch. "Now all you need are some shoes to go with it!"

Chrissy gave them another assessing look, then walked over to the shelves that held the shoes. "What size?" she called out. When Granny and Gladys replied, she grabbed some options off the shelf and returned to them. "I think these will do," she told them, handing them each a pair. "They're stylish, yet comfortable, and best of all, they don't have slippery soles. The last thing we need is you two unexpectedly ice-skating across Addie's parking lot!"

"Definitely don't need that," Gladys quipped. "I might break my hip again!" She gave Grace a wry grin, then lovingly patted her hand. "I'll stop teasing you now," she assured her.

As they tried on the shoes, Chrissy made one final trip around the store for jewelry and other accessories. By the time she was finished, Granny and Gladys looked like they'd just stepped out of a fashion magazine. As they fussed over each other's outfits, Grace pulled Chrissy aside.

"Is there any way I can pay for this without making them change back into their old clothes?" Grace whispered.

"No problem," Chrissy assured her. "I'll just cut the tags off real quick, and then you can be on your way!"

Lyda wandered over and stood near Grace. "We should do this sometime," she said, echoing Grace's earlier thoughts. "It's been a lot of fun watching those two, and Chrissy's a genius when it comes to choosing outfits for people."

"I could not agree more!"

Once they'd paid and were back in the car, Grace checked her watch. "Alright, you two, we have just enough time to drop you off at Addie's. I hope you're ready!"

"As ready as we'll ever be, dear!" Granny and Gladys replied in unison.

***

The four of them walked into Addie's Diner and looked around at all the familiar faces. It appeared half the town had shown up for lunch, despite the weather. Grace began to worry when all the tables appeared full, but then she spotted Mitchell and Vincent in a corner booth in the back.

"This way," she said, motioning for everyone to follow.

Lyda waved for them to go ahead and walked over to the counter to talk to Addie. Granny and Gladys followed, but their steps had slowed considerably. To Grace, it seemed their earlier excitement had changed to trepidation.

"It's just lunch with a couple of old men," she whispered to them. "There's nothing to be nervous about."

"Easy for you to say, you already have a man," Gladys whispered back.

Grace gave her an incredulous look. "You're eighty-one years old, you've had plenty of men in your time! Besides, this is just lunch, you're not looking to get married." She studied Gladys closely. "Or are you?"

Granny rolled her eyes and shooed them both forward. "She's right, Gladys, we can handle a couple of gentlemen."

When they reached the table, Granny and Gladys slid into the booth as Grace introduced them.

"Vincent, Mitchell, this is Gladys and my granny, Josephine."

"It's a pleasure to meet you both," Vincent said, offering his hand. When they'd finished shaking hands, it was Mitchell's turn to extend his.

"Well, I guess I'll be on my way now," Grace said as she slowly backed away from the table. When no one noticed, she pivoted and headed back to the counter where Lyda was waiting with Addie.

On her way back, she was stopped by the sound of someone calling her name. She looked around to see who it was and saw Thorne waving to her from a booth.

"Hey, Thorne," she said as she approached his booth. "Are you on your lunch break?" Why did she ask that? Of course he's on his lunch break.

Ever the gentleman, Thorne smiled up at her and ignored her awkwardness. "Actually, I'm supposed to meet Rebekah for lunch, but she hasn't shown up. You haven't seen her by any chance, have you?"

Grace tried to think back to the last time she'd seen Rebekah. Things were so crazy these days, she was having a hard time remembering. "I think I saw her last night," Grace said slowly. She nodded her head as it came back to her. "Yeah, I definitely saw her last night. But that was only because there was a problem at the hotel. I could try to call her?" Grace offered.

Thorne shook his head. "I've already tried that, a few times..." He signaled to a passing waitress, pulled a couple of bills out of his wallet, and then slid out of the booth. "I'm sure I'll catch up with her eventually. Thanks, Grace, it was good to see you again." He gave a small wave, then strode out of the restaurant.

"It was good to see you too," she called after him. That was strange. Was something going on between him and Rebekah? She would have to remember to ask the next time she saw her.

Grace continued back to the counter where Lyda and Addie were waiting.

Lyda looked up as Grace approached. "How'd it go?"

Grace glanced over her shoulder then back at Lyda. "They seem fine," she said slowly. "I don't know, I just have a weird feeling all of a sudden."

Addie placed her hand on top of Grace's and gave it a reassuring squeeze. "I'm sure it's nothing. You're just not used to seeing your granny on a date, that's all." She leaned forward so that only Grace and Lyda could hear. "What's going on at the hotel? Word around town is that Jilly got caught stealing."

The air whooshed out of Grace's lungs as she looked to Lyda, her eyes wide with panic. "Where did you hear that? Did one of those men with Granny and Gladys tell you that?"

"No," Addie replied, her forehead creasing as she struggled to remember where she'd heard the news. "I don't remember who told me, just that it was the topic of conversation this morning. Why? Is it true?"

"Of course it's not true," Grace exclaimed in a voice louder than necessary. She glanced around to see if anyone had noticed her outburst, then sheepishly turned back to Addie. "I'm sorry, I didn't mean to bite your head off. It's just—"

"—it's okay, Grace, you don't need to say anything more," Addie assured her. "What I'd like to know is why she was accused in the first place?"

How much should she tell her? Grace had been trying to make it a point not to open her big mouth. But if things were already this out of hand, was more information better than less? One thing was for sure, she could definitely count on Addie to spread whatever news Grace told her.

"One of the guests has misplaced a necklace, and she happens to be of the opinion that people in the service industry tend to be..."

"Thieves?" Addie spat out, her eyes flashing angrily. "You want to know how many times a customer has left something behind and then stormed in here accusing one of my staff of stealing it? It's like, it's not enough we wait on you hand and foot, we must also be dishonest too."

It was Grace's turn to squeeze Addie's hand. "I'm sorry," she said gently. "I didn't mean to set you off."

"It's not your fault, it just really chaps my hide to see good people accused like that. In a town this size, that kind of thing can ruin a person's reputation," Addie replied, the light bulb going off as soon as the words left her mouth. "Oh, I see, that's what you're worried about, isn't it?"

Grace nodded. "Jilly just sank all her money into buying Bea's Bakery. This is the absolute worst timing for something like this to happen."

"Leave it to me," Addie said, her expression resolute. "I'll make sure to set straight everyone who comes in here talking that nonsense."

"Thank you," Grace said, hopeful that would be enough. She took one last look at Granny, saw she was laughing, and decided it was time to go. "Watch out for those two, will you?"

Addie nodded and laughed. "Which two?" she joked.

Lyda took Grace's arm and gently pulled her toward the door. "They'll be fine," she said in her mom voice. "If we're going to have any hope of finishing the cleaning before it's time to start dinner, we need to get going."

When they reached the car, Grace turned to Lyda. "You're not the one who started the rumor, are you?" She tried to keep her voice level, but there was a hint of accusation in her tone. She knew she never should have asked when Lyda's eyes narrowed and her back became ramrod straight.

"Of course not," Lyda said through gritted teeth. "And I'm offended you feel the need to ask."

"I'm sorry," Grace said quickly. "I didn't think you'd do it intentionally, I was just worried you might have accidentally said something to the wrong person, that's all."

Her eyes remained narrow, but her posture loosened a bit. "I suppose I'll believe that. But only because I'm still new here and that sort of makes sense. However," she said as Grace began to relax, "I would appreciate it if you refrained from maligning my character in the future. I would never do something to hurt someone like that."

Grace held up her hand and made the Vulcan hand salute. "I promise," Grace said solemnly.

Lyda laughed as she shook her head. "You're a goofball, you know that?"

"I may have heard that a time or two," Grace replied, a grin spreading across her face.

"Poor Cole," Lyda said as she got in the car. "If I can't stay mad at you, he doesn't stand a chance."

Grace's mouth turned down into a pout. "I would like to believe he'll never have a reason to be mad."

"Pssh," Lyda snorted. "Just wait till the honeymoon phase is over and you have a rugrat or two running underfoot. Then we'll talk!" She put the car in drive and slowly maneuvered her way out of the parking lot. "Ready to get to work?"

"As ready as I'll ever be."

Three-Evening

Dinner was fast approaching, and Grace was starting to get nervous. While it was true Granny had texted earlier and assured her Gladys had arrived home safely, Grace had yet to see Vincent and Mitchell return to the hotel. It was possible they were out running errands. It was also possible they had joined their family at whatever outing they'd had planned for the day after their lunch was over. However, most of them had already returned. Not that it was her business what her guests spent their time on.

Lyda smacked Grace's arm with an over mitt to get her attention. "Earth to Grace," she said loudly. When Grace finally focused on her, Lyda sighed. "You need to let this go already," she admonished. "It's highly unlikely Vincent and Mitchell have kidnapped your grandmother and are on their way to Canada or something."

"Unlikely, but not impossible," Grace muttered.

"If this is how you act when your eighty-year-old granny goes on a date, I feel sorry for your future daughters," Lyda teased.

That got Grace's attention. "I thought it was the dads who are supposed to go crazy over that?"

"And yet here you are…"

Grace took a deep breath and went back to filling her savory cream puffs with salmon mousse. Lyda was not the best cook in the world, so Grace had relegated her to stirring the Coq au Vin, though she had a feeling her friend would be a genius at plating.

They were almost ready to serve the appetizers when Jackie walked in and gave Grace a disparaging look.

"In my world, the chef dresses to impress," she said with disdain as she eyed Grace's jeans, sweater, and stained apron.

"I have a hard time believing you've ever seen a chef," Grace retorted. "Almost as hard a time believing you could find your way to the kitchen, yet somehow, here you are…speaking of which, why are you here?" she asked, her annoyance clear.

Jackie sniffed. "In a place this size, it's hardly a challenge. But no matter, how about we dispense with this nonsense and get to the point: Tom has worked his charms on Rebekah, as I knew he would, and she's almost ready to return home where she belongs. The only thing standing in her way is you. So please stop being selfish, and for once in your life, do the right thing."

Grace opened her mouth to protest when Jackie held up a hand to stop her. She then reached into her purse and pulled out a checkbook. "Look, I'm going to make this really easy for you. All you have to do is name your price and consider it done." She held up her hand a second time. "This is a once-in-a-lifetime opportunity, child. I suggest you give it the consideration it deserves. Your grandmother is in poor health, and let me tell you from personal experience, medical care is not cheap. On top of that, your future husband is one bad yield away from a financial crisis. Think about what this money could do for you and your family. You could pay off the farm, hire a full-time nurse for your granny, set up college funds for your future children... the list goes on. All you have to do is give my daughter the last little shove she needs to come home."

For the third time, Grace opened her mouth to respond, but this time, Lyda stepped forward and stopped her.

"I strongly suggest you do as she says and give this some serious thought," Lyda cautioned.

"Okay," Grace stammered. She was stunned to hear Lyda of all people say that, but decided to listen in case there was something she was missing.

Jackie nodded her head toward Lyda. "Finally, someone with some sense." She put her checkbook back in her purse and pursed her lips. "My plane leaves in two days, so I'm giving you twenty-four hours to make up your mind and talk to my daughter." She turned on her heel and walked back to the door, pausing with her hand on the knob. "And Grace," she said over her shoulder, "make sure you consider *all* the implications. It's not just Rebekah's future we're discussing." With that, she turned the knob, opened the door, then closed it behind her. The only sign she'd even been there the lingering scent of her expensive perfume.

Grace attempted to return to filling her cream puffs, but her hands were shaking so badly she kept dropping the puff. After a few futile attempts, Lyda gently removed the bag of filling from Grace's hand and took over while motioning for Grace to oversee the pot of Coq au Vin.

After a few moments of silence, Lyda broke the ice. "Are you okay?"

"No," Grace said as she shook her head. Tears welled in her eyes and threatened to spill down her cheeks. "I feel like she just asked me to sacrifice one family member for another." She wiped her face with a corner of her apron and looked helplessly at Lyda. "Do you think what she said is true? About Rebekah and Cole? I'm already well aware of my situation with Granny."

Lyda was silent for a moment as she thought. "I think it's possible," she hedged. "Regardless, I think the sensible thing to do would be to talk to both Cole and Rebekah and see what they have to say. It's quite possible Jackie is exaggerating in a last-ditch effort to sway you to her side."

"That makes sense," Grace agreed. "That's going to be a difficult conversation with Cole," she mused. "What am I supposed to say? 'Hey babe, is it true we're on the verge of bankruptcy and losing everything?'"

"I don't think I'd word it quite like that," Lyda replied. "Just, you know, have a conversation. This is really something you should be talking about anyway. Especially since you're about to get married. Don't you think you should know if you're about to marry someone who's, how did she put it, one bad crop from financial ruin?"

"Yes, but..."

Lyda set the piping bag on the counter and gave Grace a hug. "Look, I know this is hard, but try to forget about this long enough to make it through dinner, okay? Then you can go home and have a talk with Cole."

Grace wiped her face again and took a calming breath. "You're right," she said as she slowly blew out her breath. "Thanks, Lyda."

"Anytime," she replied.

***

The rest of the evening had been uneventful. Audrey had been, if not happy with her meal, at least not unhappy with it. It was hard to tell with her, but Grace figured that anything less than a complaint could be considered a compliment at this point. In fact, she would have considered the evening a success if it weren't for one thing: Vincent and Mitchell still hadn't come back to the hotel. No one else seemed concerned—Lyda even continued to tease Grace about it—but she would not rest until she knew what happened to them. Actually, that wasn't true. What she really needed was to see Granny with her own eyes and know she was okay. Luckily, Grace was finally able to go home.

Before she left, she sent a quick text to Cole:

Can you meet me at the house?

Three little dots flashed before his response lit up her screen.

Already there. See you soon?

Grace was relieved to know he was home waiting for her, until she reached the parking lot and realized her car was still at home. Should she ask him to come get her? Or walk the five blocks in the cold? The cold air could help clear her head...

HONK!!

She turned her head toward the sound and saw Lyda waving to her and motioning to get in the passenger seat. Grace sent another quick text:

Be there in five

Then quickly got in the car.

"Thought I'd left ya, didn't you?" Lyda asked playfully.

"I wouldn't have blamed you if you did," Grace replied. The events of the day were weighing on her, and she felt like a crappy friend all the way around. She'd accused Lyda of starting rumors, may have been the one responsible for the rumors by running her mouth to the wrong person, and was now about to confront her fiancé and accuse him of hiding information from her. On top of that, she was actually weighing the possibility of telling her best friend to go back to a life she hated. What kind of person was she?

Lyda snapped her fingers in front of Grace's face. "Earth to Grace!"

Grace turned to look at her, her eyes blinking back into focus. "What?"

"We're here, silly," Lyda said as she pointed toward Grace's house. "Whatever it is you're thinking, I want you to know it's not true."

"How do you know?"

"Because even though I've only known you a short time, I've seen enough to know you're a good person who genuinely cares about people. So, please, push those negative feelings out of your head and go have a talk with your man. I promise you'll feel better once you do." Lyda shooed her out of the car, then waved goodbye as she drove off.

Was she right? Would Grace feel better once she talked things over with Cole? There was only one way to find out. There was just one problem—she couldn't seem to make her feet move. After a few minutes of standing in the cold, looking like a fool trying to catch a chill, Grace finally mustered up the courage to go inside.

Once inside, she heard voices in the living room and went to inspect, sure Granny and Gladys must be watching an old show or movie. She was just about to walk in the door when she recognized Vincent's voice. Stunned, she stopped in her tracks and remained hidden behind the door.

"You know, I bet you two would absolutely love Florida," Vincent said. "Especially this time of year. Imagine hanging out by the beach or pool instead of hiding inside from all this cold and snow."

Granny laughed. "That does sound nice! But this has always been our home. I can't even imagine undertaking such a move at this age."

"Nah," Mitchell chimed in. "We've helped tons of people your age move. It's kind of our specialty. All you'd have to do is get on a plane. We'd handle everything else for you, including packing up this place and selling it."

Grace tried to peek through the crack in the door frame, but all she could make out was the back of one of the men's heads.

"Oh no, I could never sell this place," Granny protested. "I have every intention of leaving it to my granddaughter when I pass."

"But won't she move out to her fiancé's farm once she gets married?" Mitchell asked.

"How do you know about that?" Granny asked, her tone slightly accusatory.

Mitchell was quick to reply. "I met Cole this morning," he explained. "He told me a little bit about his farm. Forgive me if I'm being presumptuous, it just seemed logical they would live there."

Grace clapped her hand over her mouth to keep from screaming. Mitchell had just outright lied to Granny. Not only was Vincent the one who'd met Cole, there had been no such discussion about the farm, or anything else for that matter. Just what kind of game were these two playing?

"Well, even still," Granny replied, her voice still tinged with suspicion, "this place has been in my family for generations. In fact, it was my family who built this house. I can't break with tradition now and be the one who sells it. It wouldn't be fair."

The sounds of shuffling could be heard, and Grace tried to peek through the door once more. The back of the head was gone, but she still couldn't see anything and was left to assume that someone had switched seats.

"But wouldn't that be better than your granddaughter spending the rest of your life caring for you?" Vincent asked gently. "She already has a busy life, imagine what it will be like when she's married and has kids. Instead of being a burden, you could be the fun vacation destination the family visits each year. What I'm offering is the financial freedom to live out your years in a place designed to cater to our generation."

"And you'll be doing it in the lap of luxury to boot," Mitchell said enthusiastically.

This was too much. Grace was ready to charge in there and throw these men out on their rumps, but a part of her hesitated—she wanted to hear what Granny said in response.

"Well, they do have a point," Granny replied. "What do you think, Gladys, are you ready to trade in the snow for sand and surf?"

"But what about Grace?" Gladys asked in surprise. "And Grant, Molly, and little Eliza?"

Granny hesitated for a moment. "You heard the men, we have been a bit of a burden on the kids. Me especially. And look at poor Grace. She's been running herself ragged to the point that she can't even keep up with her chores. Why, just the other day we were having to clean up after her mess! No, the men are right, we'd be better off in a place that doesn't require us to do chores, and the kids would be better off living their lives on their own."

Grace could not believe what she was hearing. Did Granny really just agree to sell the house and move to Florida? All because Grace had failed to get to the dishes the other day? She had to put a stop to this right now before they did something foolish. Her mind made up, she moved to barge into the room when two strong arms wrapped around her from behind. One of them covered her mouth, stifling her scream, the other wrapped around her waist and pulled her backwards toward the stairs.

"Shh," Cole whispered in her ear. "It's just me."

When she finally calmed down and quit fighting to get out of his arms, he let her go and, taking her hand, led her up the stairs to her room.

"I need to get back down there," she said furiously once they were behind closed doors.

"You need to do nothing of the sort," Cole argued. "Let Granny handle her business."

"But you didn't hear what I heard!" Grace protested. "Those men are trying to convince her to sell the house. And it's all because of me," she whined.

Cole sat on the edge of the bed and pulled her into his arms. "I highly doubt that, but even if it's true, it would be better to approach Granny when she's alone and we can talk privately. Barging in there like a crazed lunatic will only give them ammunition to use against you." He rubbed her back in soothing circles, patiently waiting for her to calm down.

Grace looked up at him with tears in her eyes. "I don't deserve you," she whispered.

"I don't like it when you say that," he replied. He kissed the top of her head, his arms circling her waist as he pulled her tight.

She laid her head against his chest and listened to the sound of his heartbeat. "Jackie came to see me." Tears streamed down her cheeks as she repeated everything Jackie had said. She then waited with bated breath for Cole's response, certain he was about to push her away from him at any moment.

Instead, Cole tipped her face up to look at him. "I love you," he said softly, his eyes searching hers. "Do you love me?"

"Of course!" Grace tried to sit up, but he held her in place.

"I am happy to answer any questions you have about the farm, our future, whatever it is you want to know, but please don't feel like you need to sacrifice who you are over any of it. Money is necessary, but it isn't worth your soul."

"Is it true that we're one bad crop away from financial ruin?" Grace asked, her eyes closed against the tears she couldn't seem to stop from falling.

Cole softly brushed the droplets from her cheeks. "It would hurt," he admitted. "But it's something we expect and prepare for, so no, it would not ruin us."

"So the money would help?"

He sighed. "I would be lying if I said no. However, is it worth making a deal with the devil? Absolutely not. Besides that, Rebekah is a grown woman. There is nothing you can 'make' her do, regardless of what her mother thinks."

Lyda had been right—now that she'd talked to Cole, she did feel better. "I guess I need to have a talk with Rebekah."

"I think that would be a good idea. If for no other reason than to keep her updated on her mother's antics." He leaned down and kissed her gently on the lips. "For now, I think it's time for you to get some rest. Tomorrow is another day."

"You'll stay with me?"

Cole helped her to a standing position. "There's nowhere I'd rather be."

Two-Morning

The hotel was pitch black when Grace arrived to start breakfast. No one was wandering the halls, no one was waiting to complain. After the night she'd had, it was honestly a relief, though even if she hadn't had a bad night, she still wouldn't have wanted to deal with that.

As she made her way to the kitchen, she turned on lights and did a quick survey to make sure the common areas were clean and orderly. When she reached the door to the kitchen, she was surprised to see light shining underneath the door. Had she forgotten to turn them off the night before in her haste to leave? Had one of the guests been in there searching for a late-night snack? Only one way to find out.

Grace pushed open the door and cautiously entered the room, surprised to see Vincent standing in front of the coffee machine with a somewhat desperate look on his face. "Ahem," she cleared her throat.

Startled, Vincent spun around, then clasped his hands together in a prayer position. "Grace, thank God!" he exclaimed. "I'd watched you turn this blasted machine on so many times I thought for sure I could work it myself, but, let's just say, you make it look so much easier than it is."

She stepped around him and began to fill the machine. "I'm sorry about that, I'm not used to guests beating me to the kitchen! I really need to put a couple of regular coffee machines in the dining room, just in case someone wants coffee and I'm not here."

"Most hotels have them in every room..." he replied.

Do they? She'd never stayed at a hotel before. All of the rooms at the B&B had coffee makers, but she'd thought she was being thoughtful. It was kind of deflating to discover she hadn't actually been doing anything special after all. She cleared her throat again. "I will, uh, add those to the list of things I need to change around here."

"No worries," Vincent replied nonchalantly. He moved to take his usual seat at the counter while he waited for his coffee.

Please don't cause a scene, please don't cause a scene, she muttered to herself.

"What's that?" Vincent asked, his brow raised.

Grace tried to take a calming breath, but she found she just couldn't be silent anymore. She spun on her heel and marched with more force than was necessary from the coffee maker to the counter. "I overheard you trying to convince my granny to sell our house," she seethed. "You asked me to help you find a date, not a target for a real estate scam."

"Whoa!" Vincent said, his head snapping back as if he'd been slapped. He held up his hands and turned his body away from Grace, as if to put distance between them. "I don't know what you think you heard, but I never tried to convince anyone of anything!"

"I heard you tell Granny that she should trade the snow for sun and surf, and that you could help her do it," Grace retorted.

Vincent shook his head. "Look, Grace, you've got it all wrong. Mitchell and I live in Florida and we were simply telling the gals how nice it is not to deal with snow each year. When they seemed interested, I admit we may have talked up the place where we live, but only because we like it so much. We didn't mean anything by it, I swear." He placed his hand over his heart and gave her a pleading look.

His expression was so earnest, Grace was starting to doubt what she'd thought she'd heard. It was true that she'd walked in on the middle of their discussion, so it was possible she'd missed all of the things he was now claiming were said.

As if sensing her inner turmoil, Vincent leaned forward and really laid on the charm. "Us old geezers were just trying to impress a couple of special ladies, okay? Besides that, as you'll discover when you're our age, these old bones don't like the cold!"

The coffee machine stopped gurgling, so Grace walked over and poured him a cup, grateful for a moment to collect her thoughts. His story seemed plausible, but there was something about it that just wasn't ringing true. As soon as she handed him the cup, the reason why smacked her in the face.

"Mitchell told Granny he'd met Cole yesterday morning," Grace accused. "We both know that wasn't true. You were the one who met Cole, but there was no discussion about his farm as Mitch claimed."

"How do you know he didn't meet your man?" Vincent asked innocently.

Grace scoffed. "Are you serious? You know I could just call Cole right now and settle this once and for all. Do you really want to play that game?" She pulled her phone out of her pocket and prepared to dial, but Vincent didn't seem worried, which only caused more confusion. What was going on here? Had she entered the *Twilight Zone*?

The kitchen door opened, revealing a disgruntled Audrey. "Oh, good, there you are," she said when she spotted Grace. "Once again, I looked for you last night but you were gone long before we retired for the night. What do you do, run out of here the second the last dish is loaded into the dishwasher?"

Usually, the answer was no, but in this case, that was exactly what Grace had done. She'd been in such a hurry to check on Granny, she'd forgotten to check in with Audrey before she'd left. Audrey was a very demanding guest, but she wasn't wrong—Grace had failed to do her job many times over at this point.

"I'm so sorry," Grace replied, once again on the verge of tears. "Is there something you need?"

Audrey looked her up and down and wrinkled her nose. "My children are arriving late this morning." She tossed a note card on the counter in front of Grace. "This is their favorite meal. I would appreciate it if you could have that ready to serve as soon as they arrive."

Grace looked down at the card and studied the items Audrey had scrawled across it in her chicken scratch. Her mouth dropped open as each new item revealed a request more befitting a King's Coronation Ceremony than a casual lunch in a small Midwestern town. She looked up at Audrey. "I'm sorry, but this isn't possible. There is no way I have enough time to acquire and grill enough lobster for over fifty people."

"I suggest you find a way to make it happen," she sneered. "Since the moment I arrived, there has been one disappointment after another. First you have the nerve to serve me diner food when I first arrive, then one of your staff members steals my necklace. It is your job to make the customer happy, and I AM NOT HAPPY!!" She stamped her foot, her arms stiff and straight at her side.

"That's not true," Grace protested. "Jilly had an alibi, Officer Smith already checked it out."

Audrey narrowed her eyes. "Well then I guess the only person that leaves is you, isn't it?"

Vincent stood and wrapped his arm around Audrey's shoulders. "Grace would never do that," he said soothingly. "Why don't we go relax by the fireplace in the lobby?"

That suggestion only appeared to upset her more. "I would love to, but that's another thing Ms. Too-good-to-do-her-job has failed to do."

Grace smacked her forehead when she realized Audrey meant she'd failed to start the fire. Luckily, that was an easy fix, as they'd replaced the insert with a gas one and only needed to flip a switch to turn it on. "I can fix that,"

Grace said as she ran out of the room. Moments later, she returned, a triumphant smile on her face. "The lobby is ready for you," she said sweetly. "How about I bring you some coffee and pastries while you wait on breakfast?"

"How did you get a fire started that quickly?" Audrey asked, her eyes narrowed and her mouth set in a grim line.

"It's gas," Grace explained. "All I had to do was flip a switch."

"Figures," Audrey muttered. "Of course this derelict mausoleum has a fake fireplace." She allowed Vincent to guide her to the door. "This has been the worst vacation I've ever been on."

That last part stung, but Grace didn't have time to dwell on it. As soon as they left the kitchen, she ran out the back door, around to the front of the hotel, and across the street to Bea's. "I need an assortment of at least a dozen pastries," Grace said to Bea. She leaned over and placed her hands on her knees as she tried to catch her breath. Man, she was out of shape.

"Everything okay?" Bea asked, her voice tinged with concern.

"That woman's going to be the death of me, that's all," Grace shrugged.

Bea smiled sympathetically as she handed Grace a box. "I know exactly what you mean. She has been to three cake tastings and has hated every one of them. Audrey has until this afternoon to pick something, or she's going to forgo the cake at her big anniversary party."

Grace hadn't known Bea was responsible for making the cake. According to Rebekah, some big catering outfit from the city was in charge of all the food for the party. Grace had assumed that included the cake. "Good luck, my friend." They shared a commiserating look, then Grace raced outside, around the back of the hotel, and through the employee entrance to the kitchen where she found Vincent waiting.

"Alex is doing his best to soothe Audrey, but I wouldn't dally too long, he can only do so much," Vincent informed her.

"I'm almost afraid to face her," Grace admitted sheepishly. "Is there any chance you want to take her these?" Grace motioned toward the tray of pastries she was assembling, a hopeful look on her face.

Vincent nodded. "I can do that, but only if we can agree to put that ugliness this morning behind us?"

That was the last thing Grace wanted to do, but did she have a choice? Calling out Audrey's brothers would only make her angrier, and Grace had a feeling she'd only scratched the surface of that woman's anger. No, whatever was going on with the men, it was best to leave them alone and focus on Granny instead.

Grace held out her hand. "Agreed."

They shook hands, then Vincent picked up the tray and carefully backed through the door.

Now that he was gone, Grace picked up the note card again and groaned. How on earth was she supposed to pull this off? It was time to call in the big guns. Grace pulled out her phone, sent up a quick prayer, then pressed the call button and waited.

***

Grace was just starting her first batch of crepes when Rebekah came barreling through the door, her hair disheveled, the bottom of her pajama top peeking out from underneath her coat.

"I got here as fast as I could," she said, her words coming out in a rush. "What's the emergency?" She looked frantically around the kitchen as if expecting to see a literal fire to put out.

Without a word, Grace handed Rebekah Audrey's menu 'request' for lunch, then stood back and watched the expression on Rebekah's face turn from confusion to disbelief.

"This looks similar to the menu for the anniversary party," she said, her eyes wide as she looked up at Grace. "And she wants you to serve this for lunch? Today?"

Grace nodded, then flipped her crepes. "I told her it wasn't possible, but she isn't having it. I'm worried if I don't find a way, she'll make good on her threat to cancel the party and go home early."

Rebekah's eyes almost rolled out of her head. "She's threatened that so many times, I'm convinced it's nothing more than a manipulation tactic."

"What does that mean?" Grace asked, not sure she was following.

"It means she's all bark and no bite," Rebekah replied. When Grace still didn't seem to get it, Rebekah sighed in exasperation. "She has no intention of actually canceling, she's just saying that to scare us into doing what she wants."

"Oh," Grace said as it finally dawned on her. "I suppose I should have figured that out myself, but she's been so mad about her necklace and everything else, I just assumed she was serious." She pulled the finished batch of crepes off the griddle and poured out a new batch. "It doesn't matter now," she continued. "What we need is a solution, which is why I called you. Please tell me you have one?"

Some of the anger faded from Rebekah's eyes as she realized the truth of what Grace said. "I know a guy who might be able to help, emphasis on *might*."

Grace was all ears as she gave Rebekah her full attention. "Who is he and how do we find out?"

"Well, that's where the might comes in," Rebekah explained. "He sells this kind of food out of his house. He only does it two days a week, and the only way to contact him is through his social media account where he posts the times and days he's selling." She pulled out her phone and began to scroll. "I know this kind of sounds sketchy, but I swear it was some of the best food I've ever had."

"So you've tried it?" Grace asked, her skepticism evident in her tone. She'd had to jump through hoops of fire to legally serve food in the hotel, and she was part owner of the building. Why was this rando allowed to sell food out of his house?

Rebekah gave Grace one of her no-nonsense stares. "This is our only choice. Take it or leave it."

"And if Audrey, or one of her family members, gets sick?"

"We'll cross that bridge if we come to it, but let's cross our fingers and pray we don't, okay?"

When she put it like that, Grace figured she didn't have much choice but to go along with the plan. "What do we do next?"

Her fingers flew over the phone as Rebekah typed out a message to the guy. When she was finished, she put the phone back in her coat pocket. "Now we wait."

Luckily, they didn't have to wait long. Grace was pulling the last of the crepes off the griddle when they heard Rebekah's phone ding. She quickly pulled it back out of her pocket and read the message. "We're in luck," she said, holding out her hand for a high-five. "He says we'll be buying out his entire stock for the day, but if we come pick it up, he'll be ready in a few hours."

Grace checked her watch and grimaced. That left very little time to get back to the hotel and plate the food, but somehow she would have to make it work. Maybe if both Lyda and Rebekah helped, they could get it done. "I should be ready to go in about an hour."

"Perfect!" Rebekah exclaimed. "That gives me just enough time to go home, shower, and change. While I'm there, I'll make sure breakfast is taken care of, too."

So much for Grace's talk with Granny this morning. The only thing keeping her sanity in check was the knowledge Granny was unlikely to see Vincent or Mitchell today. As long as she got to her before the anniversary party, she should be fine.

When Grace realized Rebekah was still standing there, an expectant look on her face, she tried to think back to what she'd last said. Oh yeah. "Thanks, Rebekah, I appreciate you taking care of breakfast for the house while I'm here slaving away over your guests."

Rebekah snorted, then patted Grace on the back on her way out. "That's the spirit!" she teased. She paused before the door and turned back. "Don't worry, Grace, one way or another we'll make it through this."

Grace wasn't sure she believed her, but at this point, there was no use in arguing. So, she gave her a salute, and then went back to stuffing the crepes with mascarpone cream and strawberries. It was going to be another long day. She'd better add some protein to the breakfast; she would not make it on carbs alone.

Two-Afternoon

Grace left Lyda in charge of cleaning while she snuck out of the hotel and up to the city to pick up the lobster. The last time Grace spoke to Audrey, she'd reiterated her threat, which had done nothing but increase Grace's stress levels. She currently held the steering wheel in a death grip, her back stiff as a board as she navigated the busy highway.

"You need to relax," Rebekah instructed. "Everything is fine; we're making good time and should have no problem getting back to the hotel before Audrey's kids arrive."

"I really wish you hadn't just said that," Grace muttered. "You just opened the door and invited chaos in with a big ol' giant hand wave."

Rebekah let out a low whistle. "Okay, in all the time I've known you, I don't think I've heard you this sarcastic. Or negative. What gives?" She lowered her sunglasses and gave Grace an appraising look. "And don't say it's all this mess with Audrey. It's more than that and you know it."

Despite her promise last night to Cole that she would talk to Rebekah, Grace had been avoiding that particular conversation. Whether accurate or not, it felt like they were at a crossroads, and Grace was scared to see which way Rebekah would go. If she claimed she wanted to go back to New York, could Grace be happy for her? She wasn't sure. Regardless, the conversation needed to happen, and now was as good a time as any. She glanced at Rebekah, then relayed her encounter with Jackie the previous evening.

"I see," Rebekah said cryptically once Grace was finished. "Well, I guess that answers that."

"What answers what?" Grace asked. "I'm confused. Did I miss something?"

She let out a sigh. "No, not really. I told Tom I was considering his offer, more to test him than anything. Simply put, he failed."

"I still don't get it," Grace replied, her eyebrows knitting together as she tried to process what Rebekah was saying while watching the road.

"I wanted to see just how under my mom's thumb he was," Rebekah explained. "So I lied and said I was ready to consider their proposition. And the first thing he did was run to my mom and tell her. I don't care what the offer is; I am not going to spend the rest of my life with someone who bows at my mother's feet."

Grace was relieved to hear her say that. While she was ready to admit she didn't fully understand what Rebekah was giving up, she did know in her heart that it was necessary for Rebekah's happiness. "I guess this means I won't be getting that fat wad of cash after all," she deadpanned.

Rebekah snorted. "I have considered going back to New York long enough to see my dad. If you want to scam my parents, I'll help you do it," she offered.

"I hope you're joking," Grace replied, not at all certain if she was. "I could never do something like that. I would feel guilty the rest of my life."

"Yeah, I suppose I would too," she grumbled. "But you have to admit, they have it coming after what they've done."

That was still a bit of a stretch, but Grace agreed with the sentiment. People like that rarely learned until they were hit in the pocketbook—and sometimes not even then. Considering the amount of wealth Rebekah's parents had, Grace had a feeling they fell in the latter camp.

They were silent for a moment, each lost in her own thoughts, until Grace remembered her conversation with Thorne. "Hey, what's going on with you and Thorne?"

Rebekah turned her head to look at Grace. "Nothing, why?"

Grace told her about the interaction she'd had with Thorne the previous day, then waited patiently for Rebekah to respond. She surprised her by slapping her forehead with the palm of her hand.

"I forgot all about our lunch date," she groaned. "And it's not the first time I've done that either."

"And you somehow missed all his calls as well?" Grace asked skeptically. "C'mon, Rebekah, what's really going on?"

She took a moment to gather her thoughts, her hands clenching and unclenching in her lap. "I don't know," she admitted. "All this stuff with my mom and Tom has been really confusing. I feel torn between this sense of duty my parents have ingrained in me since childhood and my desire to live my life the way I want to." Rebekah turned to stare out the passenger window. "I think I've been distancing myself from Thorne subconsciously, just in case they convince me to go back to New York."

Grace gasped as her head turned sharply to face Rebekah. "But you just said you're not going back," Grace reminded her.

"I know, and I meant it," she replied. "But that doesn't change the fact it's been a difficult few weeks and that I have acted unfairly toward Thorne. Anyway, I'll talk to him as soon as I get a free minute. I owe him an explanation. And an apology."

There wasn't much she could say to that, so Grace chose silence. No matter how much she tried to empathize with Rebekah, it was impossible for her to know what she was going through. All she could do was pray for everyone involved and lend a sympathetic ear when needed.

"I think we're here," Grace announced as she pulled up to the curb outside a two-story craftsman-style home. "What do we do now?"

She pulled out her phone. "Let me text him and let him know we're here."

While they waited, Grace surveyed the neighborhood. It looked picturesque with all the snow. Some people still had their Christmas decorations up, and she tried to imagine what it looked like at night against the sparkling white backdrop. Maybe she should bring Cole up here sometime to look at lights.

"He's ready for us," Rebekah said as she opened the car door and hopped out.

She was already halfway up the drive by the time Grace got it together enough to follow. When they reached the door, it opened, revealing a man who appeared to be in his early twenties.

"Nice to meet you," he said, holding out his hand. "They're all ready to go, all you need to do is load them."

Grace's eyes bulged at the sight of sixty styrofoam containers stacked on the man's dining room table. "Do you think it will fit in the car?" she asked out loud.

The man glanced out the front window, then back at the pile. "You should be able to fit them in the trunk. And if there's any left over, as long as the backseat is free, you should be fine."

It seemed impossible to believe, but time was ticking and they needed to move. Rebekah handed the man an envelope of cash, and they got to work loading. When the man had gone back to the house for another stack, Grace took a peek inside one of the containers, just in case. Her mouth instantly watered at the heavenly smell, so she quickly shut the container before they heard her stomach rumble. Boy, was it going to be a long drive back.

***

By some miracle, they made it back to the hotel with minutes to spare. Lyda met them at the back door, and they made quick work of unloading the trunk. Once that was done, Grace hurried to put together the trays of appetizers Audrey had requested, while Lyda and Rebekah began plating the lobster.

When the clock struck one, Grace grabbed a tray and hurried to the lobby to meet "the kids." As soon as she appeared, Audrey gave her a once-over.

"Nice of you to dress for the occasion," she sneered.

Grace was sick and tired of the woman's condescending attitude and replied without thought. "You can have your lobster, or you can have a properly dressed chef," she shot back. "There simply is no time for both."

"Hmmph." Audrey stamped her foot. "I didn't realize expecting someone to look professional while doing their job was such a hardship. Especially considering that's the bare minimum to expect."

She gave Grace a look that would normally have reduced her to a pile of mush, but Grace found she no longer cared, so she glared right back. "No, you do not get to ask—nay, demand—I meet unreasonable expectations and then complain about how I look when I do it. Expecting someone to cater a last-minute luncheon, with lobster no less, is the epitome of unreasonable."

"It's your fault I had to wait to ask last minute. If you'd been here last night like you were supposed to, you would have had plenty of time."

Alexander tried to step between the two of them, but Audrey pushed him out of the way.

"Okay, fine, I admit that I was wrong for leaving last night without checking with you first, but even if I had been here, that still doesn't change things. The stores were already closed, so it would have been no different than asking this morning." Grace raked her hands down her face. "I shouldn't have to say this, but a lobster meal for over fifty people is something you schedule weeks in advance, not hours."

Rebekah peeked in the lobby, surveyed the commotion, and attempted to grab Grace's arm and pull her back to the kitchen. But Grace was having none of it and brushed her off.

"Where I come from, all I have to do is snap my fingers and at least a dozen people would have lined up and begged for the opportunity," Audrey replied, her voice dripping with acid.

"Well, ma'am, I hate to break it to you, but this isn't where you come from," Grace spat back.

Audrey gasped. "Well, I never," she huffed. "You know what, young lady, that is it—you are not getting a tip!"

"That's fine, you probably need those quarters more than I do, anyway!"

The sound of a little bell jingling caused both women to turn their attention to the door, where a large group of people were entering. Audrey, upon seeing who it was, rushed over to greet them.

Rebekah took the opportunity to get Grace alone and pulled her off to the side by the front desk. "Are you crazy?" she whispered frantically. "You can't argue with a customer like that!" She clasped Grace's arm and gave it a shake. "She's going to fire me, and when she's done with that, she's going to leave a review for your business that is so nasty no one will touch either of us with a ten-foot pole."

Grace gave her a skeptical look. "That sounds a bit dramatic," she drawled. "I mean, you're probably right about all of that, but it's only one review. Tons of businesses have survived much worse over the years."

"Who are you and what have you done with Grace?" Rebekah practically screamed. She gave Grace another shake, her eyes wide with panic. "My Grace does not act like this. She doesn't insult her guests, nor would she be okay with even the slightest hint of negativity directed toward her. Do you remember all the things you did for me last Valentine's Day? All to avoid a bad review?"

"Oh, I absolutely remember what you put me through," Grace replied. "I just feel like there are more important things going on right now than pleasing a woman who cannot be pleased."

Audrey snapped her fingers at Grace, then once she had her attention, waved her over to the group.

Grace gave Rebekah a droll look. "If you'll excuse me, I've been summoned." She then made her way over to the group and proffered her tray of cream puffs, spanakopita, and crab-stuffed mushrooms. Once everyone had a chance to take what they wanted, Grace addressed the crowd. "Lunch should be ready in twenty minutes. If you'd like, I can get you checked into your rooms while we wait?"

A woman, who looked to be a younger version of Audrey, stepped forward. "I can only hope the rooms are nicer than the lobby," she replied. "But I fear they aren't." She handed Grace the keys to her car, then wandered over to the front desk, her eyes flitting about the room as she walked.

Seeing as Grace's hands were now full, the others laid their keys on the tray, then pushed past her to join the woman.

"Let me help you," Rebekah said as she rushed over. She quickly grabbed the tray and keys, freeing Grace to resume her front desk duties. "I know they're obnoxious, but please don't start a fight," she begged. She then blew her bangs out of her eyes. "I can't believe I'm saying that to you of all people."

"I'll do my best," Grace said sweetly. She plastered a smile on her face and returned to the desk. After a few moments of typing, which was nothing more than a petty way to make them have to stand there longer, Grace handed out keys to their rooms. "Follow me, and I'll show you the way."

The rooms were adjacent to Alexander and Audrey's room, so they didn't have to walk far. When they reached the first room, Grace unlocked it with her master key and opened the door with a flourish.

"This room belongs to Lawrence and his wife, Regina," Grace said, her voice resembling one of the models on The Price is Right.

They waited until the couple, along with one of the children, entered the room, then moved on to the next one.

"This room belongs to Cabot and his wife, Cordelia," Grace announced as she opened the door. She stepped aside to allow them room to enter, then closed the door behind her.

That left Alexandra and her husband, Preston. Grace was amused to see she'd been right, and the woman who looked like Audrey was, in fact, her daughter.

When they entered the room, Alexandra crinkled her nose and spun to face her mother. "Are you serious? *This* is where we're staying? I know you said we were slumming it, but this"—she looked around the room as if she were standing in the middle of a landfill—"this is a bridge too far."

"There's a Super 8 in the next town over," Grace deadpanned. "Perhaps you'd be more comfortable there? I heard they have coffee makers in every room!"

If looks could kill, Grace would be dead ten times over. Alexandra slammed the door in her face, leaving Grace alone in the hallway with Audrey.

"Well," Grace said enthusiastically, "that went well!" She began to walk back to the kitchen. "Lunch should be ready in about ten minutes if you want to head to the dining room."

"My children are still waiting on their luggage to be brought to their rooms," Audrey called after Grace.

"I'll get the bellhop right on that!" Grace called back. She chuckled when she heard Audrey call her a worthless cow. Oh well, there was no way this could possibly end well at this point; she might as well have some fun!

Two-Evening

"The apple doesn't fall far from the tree, does it?"

Grace looked up to see Vincent standing in her. "I'm afraid to answer that," she replied. "Is this a trap?"

Vincent laughed and took a seat at what had fast become 'his spot' at the counter. "I love my family, but there's a reason I live in Florida and they live in New York."

If Audrey were her sister, Grace would live in another state too. But she felt it would be rude to say that, so she tried to come up with a safer topic since it appeared Vincent planned to stay awhile. "Tell me about Florida?" she asked, figuring that was as neutral a topic as possible.

"Well," he began, his hand going to his chin as he looked off into the distance. "It's hot, humid, crowded, expensive...basically everyone's definition of paradise!" he said with a laugh. "Seriously, though, if you love the water, there's no better place than Florida."

They were silent for a moment as Grace concentrated on the scallops she was searing for that night's Coquilles Saint-Jacques. She'd found an interesting recipe she'd wanted to try, and figured now was as good a time as any to give it a go. It would either be a hit and help her win back favor with Audrey, or it would flop and she would continue to hate her. Either way, she figured she couldn't lose.

When the silence dragged on too long, Grace cleared her throat. "Now that the kids are here, are there any big plans for tomorrow?" The last thing she needed was to be blindsided a second time. Although she did have to admit the lobster had been amazing. Even Alexandra had seemed to like it, her mood improving the tiniest bit when she'd taken her first bite. At least, that's what Grace had tried to convince herself of as she'd watched from the little window in the kitchen door. After her earlier outburst, her senses had returned, and she now felt a huge sense of shame and guilt for her behavior.

"As far as I know, the men are on babysitting duty and will be taking the kids out to museums and a discovery center, while the women go to a spa," Vincent informed her. "We're also supposed to have lunch at some French restaurant, so I'm pretty sure you're off the hook if that's what you're wondering."

Grace looked up in time to see him smile. "Am I that obvious?"

"We all heard your fight with Audrey," he replied. "That comment about the two quarters was especially entertaining!"

She winced at the reminder. That had been particularly rude and unnecessary, but she'd been so mad it had just slipped out without thought. At this point, Grace was no longer able to fathom why Audrey hadn't followed through with her threat to cancel the party and go home.

"I need to apologize for that," Grace said sheepishly.

"Don't," Vincent said firmly. "If you want to earn her respect, the last thing you should do is apologize."

That seemed like the opposite of how to earn respect, but what did she know? Should she even take his advice? She still wasn't convinced he hadn't been trying to scam Granny last night, nor had she had the opportunity to talk to Granny about it. She supposed she could always apologize later.

Audrey chose that moment to walk in, Alexandra in tow. "Oh good, you're actually here," Audrey snarked. "I've invited a couple of guests to dinner tonight, so make sure to set a couple of extra places."

Who on earth did Audrey invite, and how did she even manage to pull it off? She didn't know anyone in town, and Grace highly doubted she invited some of the locals. Nor was it likely Audrey just happened to run into some friends who were also vacationing in Winterwood. Then it hit her. There were only two people in town Audrey could possibly be referring to, and that was Tom and Jackie. Hadn't Audrey already invited Tom once?

"This isn't a restaurant," Grace reminded her. "I make enough food to feed the guests that are staying here, no more, no less." That wasn't true. She always made extra, just in case, but man, she was sick and tired of all these last-minute demands.

Alexandra opened her purse, then tossed a couple of twenties on the counter. "This should cover the extra cost," she sneered. "My gosh, I can't imagine being so poor you have to nickel and dime everything to death." She glanced at Grace and took in her faded jeans, old sweatshirt, and stained apron. "Although I guess for some that's just a way of life."

Grace opened her mouth to tell Alexandra exactly what she could do with her money, but Vincent chimed in first.

"Whoa, you two," Vincent said. "How about you lay off Grace, okay? After all, you don't mess with the cook, remember?" He kept his words light, but his tone was firm.

Even though she didn't trust him, Grace had never been more grateful to the man than she was now. The two women had no idea just how close they'd come to wearing their dinner. Which would have been a shame since she'd worked so hard on it.

Alexandra shrugged and left the room, this time Audrey following after one last dirty look lobbed in Grace's direction.

"Thank you," Grace said once they were gone. "I shouldn't let them get to me, but it's hard."

"I wouldn't take it personally," he replied. "Money makes certain aspects of life easier, but it brings with it a new set of problems. The world they live in is ruthless, and I highly doubt any of them are ever actually happy. Although, after observing you over the last few days, I'm not sure you're entirely happy either."

"Aren't you part of that world?" Grace asked, completely ignoring that last part. It didn't seem necessary to point out the only reason she wasn't happy was because of him and his family.

Vincent shook his head. "Mitch and I never really fit in, so after high school, we joined the military, and after that, we decided to continue making our own way in the world."

"But you must have remained close, right? I mean, you are here to help celebrate their anniversary."

"Family means different things to different people," he said cryptically. He pushed the stool back and stood. "I better get out of your hair. Nice chatting with you, Grace."

She watched him go, more confused than ever as to what was really going on with him. She really needed to talk to Granny, and was determined to do it tonight, no matter what she had to do to make it happen.

***

Grace was finally ready to go home, and had just reached her car when Jackie stepped out of the shadows. "Are you trying to give me a heart attack?" Grace exclaimed. "And why are you waiting around in the cold?"

"I was in my car," Jackie said with an eye-roll. "You need to pay better attention to your surroundings," she admonished.

She wasn't wrong, so Grace decided to let her have that little win. "Look, I'll spare us both the annoyance of this conversation by giving you your answer. I spoke to Rebekah, and she plans to go back to New York to see her father. Beyond that, I believe she plans to continue building her life here. I'm sorry that isn't the answer you were hoping for, but that's all I have for you."

Jackie's lips curled downward into a frown. "You're the first person I have ever met in my entire life who didn't have a price."

"That is one of the saddest things I've ever heard," Grace said softly. "Your daughter is not for sale, nor should you want her to be."

"There are some things you just can't understand until you have children of your own," Jackie replied, her tone wistful. "You spend nine months carrying this...being inside your body. You dream of her and all the things you're going to do together long before she's even taken her first breath. And then you meet your precious baby for the first time and all those dreams suddenly feel so real—so possible. But then your sweet baby grows up and with one single decision dashes all of your hopes and dreams."

Grace could sympathize to a point, but it was a small point. "Rebekah is still your baby," she pointed out. "She isn't trying to hurt you; she just has her own hopes and dreams. If you would just give her a chance, I know she would love to include you in them."

For the briefest of moments, Grace had a glimmer of hope she'd actually gotten through to Jackie. But then a car pulled up and broke the spell.

"Hey, Grace?" Thorne called out as he rolled down his window. "Is Rebekah here? I've been looking all over for her, but I can't find her."

"She was, but she left for the house about five minutes ago," Grace called back.

Thorne nodded his thanks, rolled up his window, then drove off, leaving Grace and Jackie alone again.

"Who was that man?" Jackie asked.

"That's Rebekah's boyfriend. You met him at the Christmas festival in the park," Grace reminded her.

"I see. Well, I guess we're done here." Jackie pulled her coat tighter around her and walked to the driver's side of her car. "I hope you don't come to regret this. You could have become a very rich woman."

Grace sighed. "My bills are paid, I have enough food to feed my family, and I'm surrounded by people I love and care for, so, in my opinion, I'm already the richest woman in the world."

Without another word, Jackie got in her car and drove off, leaving Grace to finally go home. As she was pulling out of the parking lot, she realized she'd forgotten to check in with Audrey again. Oh well, she'd just have to take the risk that Audrey had more surprises in store for her.

As soon as she got home, she rushed to Granny's room, relieved to see she was still awake.

"What's all the fuss about?" Granny asked, giving Grace a curious look.

Now that she was here, she wasn't sure how to broach the subject. If she outright asked about what she'd overheard, then Granny would know she'd been eavesdropping. Since that wasn't a good look, Grace decided to play it safe.

"I've been dying to hear about your date!" she said brightly.

Granny chuckled and patted the bed beside her. "We had a lovely time," she told Grace. "So lovely that when we finished lunch, the guys came back here so we could continue our conversation."

"I guess that explains the car parked outside when I got home last night," Grace said, subtly attempting to prod Granny in the right direction.

"The day got away from us," she explained. "Gladys and I haven't had that much fun in ages!"

"Did you talk about anything interesting?" Grace tried to prod her again, her patience fading as she desperately wanted to talk about what she'd overheard.

Granny shook her head. "Nothing that would interest you, dear. Just old people talk."

While Grace may not be old, she did not consider selling one's house and moving to another state to be 'old people talk.'

"Spit it out, Grace," Granny said sternly. "I can see you have something to say, so might as well say it."

"I overheard you talking about moving to Florida," Grace spit out. There, she'd said it. Now Granny had no choice but to address it.

To her surprise, Granny simply laughed and patted her hand. "Is that what this is all about? We were just talking about how nice it would be to spend winters somewhere warm. I think they call people who do that 'snowbirds.' Anyway, I'm not going anywhere, so put that out of your head."

This was not at all the way this conversation was supposed to go. Grace knew what she heard, but now both Vincent and Granny were denying it. Why? What was going on? Or had she really just misunderstood the whole thing? She had been busy and stressed lately; was it possible her mind was playing tricks on her? Since she couldn't know for sure, what could she do?

Granny let out a big yawn and stretched out her arms. "I think it's past my bedtime. And yours from the look of it." She gave Grace a hug and patted her cheek. "Get some sleep, Grace, you need it."

Grace nodded, then got up to leave. As she reached the door, something on the dresser caught her eye and she paused long enough to see what it was: a large folder with a real estate logo embossed in big, glossy letters. So, she wasn't crazy after all. She hurried out of the room and up the stairs where she called Cole.

"You won't believe what I just found," she blurted out when he answered.

"What's that?"

She spent the next five minutes recounting everything that happened that day, then finally paused to see what he had to say about it.

"Baby, do you really think Granny would sell the house and move several states away without telling you?"

"If she thought she was doing it for my own good, she might," Grace said angrily. "Do I need to remind you of what she had planned last Christmas? She wouldn't even be here right now if—" She trailed off, the words too difficult to say out loud. "I'm just worried," she said, her voice so low it was practically a whisper. "Something is wrong, I can feel it."

Cole let out a breath. "Would you like me to come over?"

"I always want you to come over," she quickly replied.

"I'll be there in ten minutes. I'm not sure what we should do, but we'll figure something out, okay?"

"Thank you," Grace said before ending the call. She rubbed the back of her neck, the tension refusing to loosen. She had just enough time to shower and change before Cole arrived, so she decided to focus on that instead.

Somehow, things would be okay. They had to be.

One-Morning

Despite getting more sleep than usual, Grace was exhausted. It was finally New Year's Eve, the day everyone had been waiting for, and all she wanted to do was spend the day in bed. There were only two more days to go—three if you count the day everyone checked out and went home—and she was counting down the seconds. She really needed a vacation. Could they go on the honeymoon first and do the wedding second? Okay fine, that was a silly thought, but still.

Once again, the hotel lobby was dark, and this time the kitchen was as well. No Vincent roaming the halls to escape his brother's snoring, no Audrey waiting to jump out and surprise her with a last-minute request of wagyu steaks for fifty people. Although, that last one could still happen.

In blessed silence, she started the coffee machine, then opened the doors to the fridge and prayed for inspiration. Sadly, none came. She really wanted to do something special for the holiday, but since she'd spent the last five days attempting one fancy meal after another, she was all tapped out. Would the guests settle for scrambled eggs and toast? Alexandra's face popped into her head, sour expression and all. No, that would simply not fly. She shut the doors, then moved to the pantry, but still nothing came.

Well, there was only one thing left to do, so Grace pulled out her phone and googled fancy breakfast ideas for large crowds. As she scrolled through the list, an idea began to form. The hotel kitchen had come fully stocked, and while a lot of the items had been outdated, she had saved all the glassware. Which meant she had enough champagne flutes to serve the guests several times over.

Her plan now fully formed, Grace began to frantically pull items out of cupboards and line them up on every available surface. When she was done, she stepped back and surveyed the mess. "This could actually work," she mumbled.

"Champagne for breakfast?" Vincent asked, his head cocked as he looked around the room. "Audrey finally broke you, didn't she?"

A burst of laughter erupted from somewhere deep in her chest. Had Audrey 'broken' her, or had she inspired her? Grace chose to believe it was the latter.

"I'm serving yogurt parfait for breakfast and thought it would look pretty layered in champagne flutes," Grace explained. "I'm also making egg cups with spinach, feta, and bacon."

"That sounds like a lot of work," Vincent mused. "Will you be able to get it done before the vultures descend?"

Grace laughed again at the image he'd painted. "Lyda should be here any minute, so between the two of us, I think we'll be fine." She walked over to the coffee machine and poured him a cup, certain that was the real reason he was there.

When she handed it to him, he gratefully accepted and let out a deep sigh as he took his first sip. "That hits the spot every time!" Instead of pulling out the stool, he turned to leave. "I'm going to get out of your hair," he announced as he headed toward the door. "Looking forward to seeing your creations!" He waved over his shoulder as he exited.

As Vincent went out one door, Lyda came in the other. "Sorry I'm late," she said as she pulled off her gloves and coat. She gave Grace a dry look. "Since the kids aren't here, I honestly have no excuse other than I really didn't want to get out of bed this morning."

"Cole had to practically shove me," Grace admitted with a laugh. "I was just thinking about how badly I need a vacation, but since that's not happening anytime soon, we need to schedule our little date at Chrissy's. We need something to look forward to!"

"Tell me when and I'll be there," Lyda replied. She glanced at the counters, then did a double-take. "I'm not surprised these people have driven you to drink, but this seems a bit excessive," she joked.

Grace explained her plan, relieved when Lyda nodded along in agreement.

"If that doesn't scream 'fancy' at this point, I don't know what will," Lyda declared.

While Lyda filled the champagne flutes with alternating layers of Greek yogurt, granola, and berries, Grace went to work on the egg cups. Once the first batch was in the oven, Grace began to doubt her plan.

"Do you think this will be enough food?" she asked Lyda. "I mean, it's cute and all, but I fear they're going to need at least two of everything, maybe even three to feel full."

"We could call Bea and see if she has any muffins left," Lyda suggested.

The fact that Lyda didn't disagree only fueled Grace's fears more. Since her suggestion to call Bea made sense, she gave her a call while she assembled the next batch of egg cups.

"Hey, Bea," Grace said once Bea answered her call. "Any chance you have any muffins?"

"Sure, darlin'," she replied in her usual cheerful tone. "I'll get 'em boxed up if you want to run over and pick them up?"

Grace gave Lyda a thumbs up. "Sounds great, I'll be right there." She ended the call, then turned to Lyda. "I shouldn't be long, but just in case the timer goes off before I get back, all you have to do is swap batches and then reset the timer for fifteen minutes."

"No problem," Lyda said, giving a mock salute. "Just try your best not to get sucked into the latest gossip, okay?"

It was Grace's turn to give the salute before taking off at a run for Bea's. She was very fortunate the bakery was right across the street from the hotel—something she couldn't help but think each time she made a mad dash over there. When she rushed in, she found Bea still boxing up muffins.

"Goodness!" Bea exclaimed. "I've barely had a chance to box up the blueberries."

"I should have asked how many you have," Grace wheezed. Between the cold and the running, she was finding it hard to catch her breath.

Bea did a quick count of the muffins in the case. "I have twenty blueberry, twenty cinnamon streusel, twenty apple, and fifteen banana nut."

That was only seventy-five, but it would have to do. "Great! I'll take them all," Grace informed her.

"Terrible business about Jilly and Jenny," Bea said, shaking her head. "I was really hopeful the two of them would work things out."

"What do you mean?" Grace asked in surprise. She knew Jenny wasn't happy Jilly bought the bakery, but that was hardly earth-shattering news.

"Jenny's the one who spread the rumor Jilly's a thief," Bea explained. "Now at least half the town is mad at Jenny, and the other half is wary of Jilly and claiming they plan to boycott the bakery once I officially hand over the keys. It's just sad business all the way around."

"But how did Jenny—" Grace stopped mid-sentence as the answer practically smacked her in the face. Jenny and Officer Smith were dating. Of course, she heard all about it from him and then used that as an opportunity to hurt Jilly. Grace was shocked by how perfect of a storm it was. She was also shocked by how vindictive Jenny had turned out to be. As long as Grace had known her, she'd always been a kind and friendly woman. Grace understood she was upset, but she was taking it out on the wrong person. It wasn't Jilly's fault Bea decided to sell to her instead.

When Bea was done loading the boxes, Grace gratefully accepted them. "I really hope things work out for everyone," she finally replied. "If there's anything I can do…"

"I've done what I can, but I think we're going to have to let this one work itself out," Bea said sadly. "Enjoy your muffins!"

Grace nodded, then returned to the hotel, this time at a more reasonable pace. When she entered the kitchen, Lyda was waiting, her hands open as she took the boxes from Grace.

"I'll start setting up the buffet," Lyda volunteered. "If we're quick, we should be able to get it done before the first guest comes down."

"Sounds good," she replied, though her mind was a million miles away. There was simply too much going on for her to concentrate on any one thing. Since she couldn't solve the Jilly problem, or the Rebekah problem, or even the Audrey problem, that left the situation with Vincent, Mitchell, Granny, and Gladys. While she and Cole had failed to come up with a solution the night before, there was one person who might be able to help. All she had to do was find a few spare minutes to talk to him. Too bad that was easier said than done.

***

Grace's chance to escape came when the guests decided to leave earlier than expected. As they drove one way out of town, she went another. Not that it mattered if anyone saw her leave; she just didn't want to get accused of shirking her duties again—which she was in no danger of doing, by the way. Once she'd explained her suspicions to Lyda, she'd happily volunteered to stay behind and get a jump on the cleaning. While she was gone, Grace would have to remember to ask Emilio to give Lyda a raise. The woman was practically a saint and deserved every penny they could afford to pay her.

When she arrived at Grant's office, she was surprised, and a little alarmed, to see that Molly's car still wasn't there. She became even more concerned when she plopped into a chair in front of Grant's desk and saw just how ragged and sleep-deprived he looked.

"Oh my gosh, Grant, is everyone okay? Eliza? Molly? You?" She leaned forward, almost afraid to breathe as she waited for his response.

"We're fine," he said, rubbing his eyes with the back of his hands. "Eliza's been fine for days now, but Molly has become so obsessed with her getting sick again she made herself sick from the stress."

"It sounds like we might need to stage an intervention," Grace replied, her heart going out to them. If Molly was even half as miserable as Grant appeared, things were much worse than she'd imagined.

Grant snorted. "Good luck," he said, his voice bitter. "We've had multiple talks with the pediatrician, she's talked to every mommy friend she has at least three times, and poor Gladys has tried too many times to count to get through to her. All have failed." He sighed and ran a hand through his hair. "What she really needs is a good old-fashioned distraction. Something she can really sink her teeth into."

"Oh," Grace said, perking up. "In that case, do I have just the thing for you!"

The look Grant gave her was a cross between disbelief and desperation. "I'm honestly afraid to ask," he replied. "But please, tell me what you've got."

Grace laid it all out for him in as much detail as possible. By the time she'd reached the part where she'd found the real estate packet on Granny's dresser, she could tell she'd piqued his interest, but not to the extent she'd been hoping. "So, what do you think? Can you help?"

"What exactly is it you want me to do?" he asked. He leaned back in his chair and steepled his fingers as he thought about what she'd said. "I can see why you're concerned, but telling someone they should move to a warmer climate isn't exactly a crime."

"I feel like you're missing the part where they claimed they could handle it all themselves," she reminded him, "as well as the part where they encouraged Granny not to talk to me about it. Don't you think that's suspicious?"

Grant shrugged, then shouted for Emilio to join them. When he entered the office and took a seat next to Grace, Grant explained the situation in a far more concise way than Grace had. "What do you think about all this?"

Emilio cleared his throat. "I've heard of scams similar to this before," he said slowly. "It's possible these guys are trying to pull a fast one, but you don't really see this kind of thing from wealthy people—especially ones from prominent families. It would draw too much scrutiny."

That made sense, and Grace had questioned that part herself. In fact, it was partly why she kept questioning herself. However, she still felt they weren't taking this as seriously as they should be.

"They want Gladys to sell her house too," Grace informed Grant. "So unless you want to find yourself out on the street with the rest of us, you may want to devote some time to ensuring this truly isn't a scam."

Grant sat up straight and grabbed a pen and pad of paper. "Do you remember the name of the company you saw on the folder?"

Grace pictured the folder in her mind. "Silver Keys Realty."

He scribbled the name on a piece of paper. "Is there anything else you can tell me about these Vincent and Mitchell characters?"

Luckily, she'd planned ahead and had already written down all the information she had. She reached into her purse, pulled out the note card, and slid it across the desk to him. "It's possible some, if not all, of that is fake, but it's everything I was given when they made reservations at the hotel."

Grant reached for the note card, studied it a moment, then nodded. "This is enough to get started. I'll see if I can convince Molly to research the men while Emilio and I tackle the financial history of the real estate company. With any luck, the thought of losing her home will be enough to snap Molly out of her funk and spur her into action."

"What should I do in the meantime?" Grace asked, relief flooding her senses. She could feel the tension literally releasing from her neck as hope replaced her fear for the first time since she'd overheard the conversation between Granny, Gladys, Vincent, and Mitchell the other night.

"I want you to go on pretending everything is fine," Grant instructed. "We don't want you to do anything that might make them react rashly."

"If they think she's onto them, that might make them abandon ship, so to speak," Emilio pointed out.

Grace considered that. "That would keep Granny and Gladys safe, but what about their next victims?"

"If this is a scam—and I'm still not convinced it is," Emilio replied, "this kind of thing is going to take a long time to investigate and prove. And that's not including the time it will take for the proper government bodies to get involved and do their own investigation." He held up his hand when Grace looked like she wanted to protest. "I'm not saying we let them get away with it, I'm just saying protecting Granny and Gladys needs to be our first priority."

"I agree," Grant said firmly. "But there's something else we need to consider—your guests are scheduled to leave in less than two days. I have no idea how long this con usually takes, but I imagine they'll need to wrap it up soon."

"Soon, as in, tonight?" Grace asked, her fear doubling at the realization that Vincent and Mitchell had likely planned this all along. And she had been an unwitting accomplice.

Grant nodded. "Like I said, there's still a very real chance this is all a misunderstanding. I'm just suggesting we remain vigilant as a precaution, okay?"

No, it really wasn't okay, but what else could they do? It wasn't like she wanted the men to be scammers—in fact, she was very much hoping they weren't. She liked Vincent and wanted to believe this was nothing more than a simple misunderstanding on her part. But in the event they were con men—well, if that ended up being the case, she felt she had a duty to do whatever she could to stop them. Unfortunately, there didn't appear to be much she could do.

A quick glance at her watch showed she'd been there longer than planned, so she grabbed her purse and prepared to leave.

"Hang in there, Grace," Grant called out as she left his office.

She gave him a wave, then braced herself for the shock of cold she would receive once she opened the door and hurried to her car. Things were out of her control, so nothing to do now but head back to the hotel and clean. Although... while there was nothing she could do to help Granny, there was still one thing she could do to help Jilly.

Grace pulled out her phone, scrolled through her contacts, then pushed the call button. It was time for a treasure hunt!

One-Afternoon

R iley showed up just after noon, all smiles as he pulled his metal detector out of the bed of his truck. "You must have done an awful lot of sweet talking to convince boss man to give me the afternoon off!" he said to Grace when he met her in the lobby.

"Nah, I'd say he owes me for all the months I've shoveled poop for him!" Grace said with a laugh.

Lyda walked in from the dining room and glanced between them. "What did I miss?"

"Just a joke about poop," Grace said with a shrug. She turned to Riley. "What do you need from me to get started?"

"All I need is to know where to start."

Grace looked around the lobby, but there didn't seem to be many places the necklace could hide there. She'd already checked the chairs and under the tables, but he might as well scan those too, just in case. "Here is good," she replied. "Then you're free to make your way through the hotel as you see fit. The bedrooms are unavailable, but everywhere else is fair game."

"Sounds good, I'll let you know if I find anything."

It was tempting to follow Riley around and watch him work—Grace had never seen a detectorist in action before—but alas, there was still so much work to be done. So, she left him to it and followed Lyda back to the kitchen.

"What's left on the to-do list?" Lyda asked. She clasped her hands behind her back and began to rock on her feet as she waited for Grace to answer. "Nice job with breakfast, by the way, everyone seemed to enjoy it, including she-who-shall-not-be-named!"

"The boys must be on a Harry Potter kick," Grace joked. "Unfortunately, while I'm happy the guests liked my little champagne gimmick, we now have over a hundred champagne flutes to wash."

Lyda eyed the tubs full of carefully stacked glasses. "Any chance they can go in the dishwasher?"

Could they? Grace wasn't entirely sure. She decided to Google it, then looked at her phone in dismay when she saw the results. "It says they can only go in the dishwasher if they're plastic or glass made specifically for that purpose. Considering their age, I'm afraid hand washing is in our future."

"Well," Lyda said as she rolled up her sleeves, "might as well get to it."

As they continued to survey the mountain of glass, Rebekah stormed in.

"There you are!" She said to Grace. "You will not believe what my mother is trying to do now!"

Jackie rushed in, Tom hot on her heals.

"Rebekah Ann Rutherford, how dare you walk away from me when I'm talking to you!" Jackie seethed.

Rebekah tossed up her arms in frustration. "I can't take this anymore," she screamed. "I want my life back. The life I had before these two came to town and tried to dismantle everything I've worked so hard to build for the sole purpose of turning me into some trophy wife that gets cheated on and ignored until he"—she pointed to Tom—"needs to parade me around in front of investors!"

Grace and Lyda exchanged glances, their eyes wide in surprise at the scene playing out in front of them.

"C'mon, Rebekah, that's not fair," Tom replied, his usual amused expression replaced by one of consternation. "I would never do that to you."

"That's what they all say," Rebekah yelled. "Until they do."

Jackie reached out a hand and tried to touch Rebekah's arm, but she yanked it back and out of her reach. "That's the exact kind of life you had with Daddy. Can you honestly say you were happy with that?" When Jackie didn't respond, Rebekah continued. "That's what I thought. So why on earth do you want that kind of life for me?"

"Rebekah!" Jackie reared back as if she'd been slapped. "I—"

Thorne entered the kitchen from the dining room, then stopped dead in his tracks when he saw the group gathered inside. His eyes went to Rebekah as a pained expression crossed his face. "It looks like I finally found you," he said softly. "But I guess now's not a good time." He turned to leave, paused for a moment, then ran a hand through his hair as if wrestling with himself. Finally, as if making up his mind, he turned back. "No, you mean too much to me to give you up without a fight."

He crossed the room, took Rebekah's hand in his, then got down on one knee. "Rebekah, I know we started off on the wrong foot, and that was one hundred percent my fault," he added quickly, "but you are the best thing that has ever happened to me, and if you'll let me, I will spend every day for the rest of my life proving to you just how much I love you. Will you please do me the honor of becoming my wife?"

Grace, Lyda, Jackie, and even Tom gasped, their eyes riveted to the couple in front of them.

Rebekah began to shake her head as tears stung her eyes. "I'm sorry, but no, I can't."

Thorne's eyes began to water as his face filled with anguish. "Okay," he whispered, his voice breaking. "I won't bother you again." He rose to his feet, every step toward the door weighted with regret. His head was bowed as he left the room, his steps slow, as if part of him still held out hope Rebekah would change her mind and call him back.

When he was gone, Rebekah turned to her mother, her expression full of bitterness and anger. "Are you happy now? That man could have been my future. We could have lived happily ever after together." She let out a loud wail, her fists clenching at her sides.

Jackie reached out again, but Rebekah slapped her hand away. "Go home, please," Rebekah begged. "I never want to see you again." She looked at Tom. "Either of you." A sob escaped her throat as she ran toward the door, her eyes so full of tears she struggled to find the knob. Once she did, she left as fast as her legs would carry her.

Grace's chest ached as she watched her go. She couldn't help but wonder if she had just witnessed the ending of a love story. That thought lingered in the heavy silence.

"I failed her, didn't I?" Jackie asked softly. "I was so sure I knew what was best for her, it never crossed my mind I could be wrong."

"It's our job to love them," Lyda said gently. "The rest is up to them."

Jackie closed her eyes and bowed her head. "It's time for me to go home." She took Tom's arm and allowed him to lead her out of the kitchen.

When they reached the door, Tom paused to wave goodbye, then disappeared, likely for the last time.

For a moment, neither woman spoke. The kitchen felt impossibly quiet, heavy with unspoken words. Then Riley strolled in, cheerfully oblivious to the storm that had just passed.

He looked at them for a moment, then glanced around the room in confusion. "Did something happen? You two look like you just found out someone died." A horrified look came over his face. "Oh my gosh, did someone actually die? Because if they did, I didn't mean to be disrespectful or anything."

"It's okay, Riley," Grace assured him. "No one died. We just witnessed a very sad moment between a very broken family."

"Oh," he muttered under his breath. "That's almost as bad."

Grace happened to agree with him on that, but there was still work to be done, so she needed to try to put that stuff out of her mind and concentrate on the present. "Did you find anything?" she asked hopefully.

Riley held out his hand and displayed a small pile of coins, a couple of old bottle caps, and what looked like the car from the Monopoly game Grace played with the kids at Thanksgiving. Grace laughed when she saw it. "That's the one the kids always fought over," she said softly, a pang of nostalgia tugging at her heart. What wasn't there was a necklace.

"There's one more place to look, but we have to be careful to only detect behind furniture and under the bed and tables, okay?" Grace asked. When Riley nodded, she led him out of the kitchen and down the hall to Audrey and Alexander's room. "I know I said the bedrooms were off-limits, but since this one belongs to the Bellamys, it makes sense to check here. Just be careful not to disturb their things."

As Riley ran the detector over all the places the necklace could have conceivably fallen or rolled, Grace watched in fascination. He was wearing headphones, so she couldn't hear any beeping, but it was still exciting to witness him move the instrument around the room. At one point, the machine let out a faint buzz near the radiator, making Grace's heart leap, but it turned out to be nothing more than an old nail lodged in the floorboards. After a couple more passes, he took off the headphones and shook his head.

"There's nothing," he announced. "Sorry, Grace, but the necklace does not appear to be in the hotel. At least not in any of the places I've looked."

That was extremely disappointing. She was really hoping she could present the necklace to Audrey that night, followed by a huge "I told you so," as well as a demand for an apology for falsely accusing Jilly. What was worse was that since they didn't find the necklace, that meant there were only two possibilities left for what happened to it: either Audrey was lying and it was part of some sort of insurance scam, or one of her relatives stole it. Both could prove to be troublesome.

"Thanks, Riley," Grace said as she walked him out. "I know we didn't find the treasure, but I hope you at least had fun."

"I'm always looking for a reason to give ol' Bessie a whirl," Riley replied. "Thanks for letting me poke around. And for getting me a few hours off work!"

Grace laughed as she waved goodbye. She stared out at the snow for a moment, then turned back to the kitchen. It was time to tackle the rest of the chores. Only forty-eight hours to go and this would all be over. She could handle that.

***

There wasn't a lot of time before Grace was supposed to help Granny and Gladys get ready for the party, but she couldn't stand waiting another minute to check on

Rebekah. She had no idea where Rebekah had gone after the earlier fiasco, but the only place she knew to look was at the house, so that's where she went. When she saw Rebekah's car parked in the driveway, Grace let out a sigh of relief.

She parked her car on the side of the road, rushed inside and up the stairs to Rebekah's room, pausing just long enough to grab a box of tissues from the bathroom counter. When she reached the door and saw it was closed, she briefly debated knocking, then slowly opened it to reveal Rebekah huddled in the middle of the bed. Grace slid onto the bed beside her and wrapped her arms around her trembling friend.

"Want to talk about it?" Grace asked gently.

Rebekah let out a sob as tears continued to stream down her cheeks. "What's there to say?" she choked out. "Other than I just ruined the best relationship I've ever had."

Grace grabbed a handful of tissue out of the box and handed it over. "How about why you said no? This doesn't seem like the reaction of someone who didn't want to get engaged."

"He was only asking me to stop me from leaving," Rebekah said bitterly. "Not because he actually wants to marry me."

"Are you sure?" Grace asked, memories of the look of anguish on Thorne's face when Rebekah said no filling her mind. "Because he didn't look like a man who was only proposing out of some sense of duty or fear, or whatever it is you think he was doing it out of."

Rebekah turned to face Grace. "They got to him," Rebekah argued. "It's the only thing that makes sense. He would have had no other reason to propose when he did if it wasn't because he was afraid I was going to leave him to go back to New York."

"And that's not a sign of love?" Grace asked in surprise. "I mean, he could have just wished you the best of luck in your future endeavors and waved goodbye as you left. Instead, he frantically chased you all over town and then did the one thing he could to show you how much you mean to him."

"Yeah, that sounds romantic when you put it that way, but just once I wish someone would ask me what I want, you know?" She wiped her eyes and then blew her nose. "All everyone has done since my mother arrived is try to make decisions about what's best for me."

Grace wasn't sure she agreed. Thorne had asked, and had quickly accepted Rebekah's decision. No fighting or pleading had occurred. But Rebekah did not appear to be in a place to hear that, so Grace changed tactics. "Okay, what do you want?"

Surprised, Rebekah looked up into Grace's eyes. "I want to stay here and build my career as the best event planner in the Midwest."

"Is that all?"

"And I want to marry Thorne," Rebekah sobbed.

Grace wrapped her arms around Rebekah's shoulders and gently rocked her while she cried. There had to be a way to fix this. Somehow, she would find a way.

They stayed that way for a while, each lost in their own world. Suddenly, Rebekah shot straight up in bed and frantically looked around the room.

"Oh my gosh, what time is it?" Rebekah gasped.

Grace checked her watch. "Almost three," she replied, her eyes widening as she remembered the party was supposed to start at six.

Rebekah scrubbed at her face and drew in a shaky breath. "I can't fall apart now. If I do, they win." She hopped off the bed, rushed over to the mirror, and began to swiftly fix her hair and makeup. When she was finished, she gave Grace a quick hug. "I've got to get back to the winery. Will I see you there?"

"No." Grace shook her head. "I'm not on the guest list," she added with a shrug. "Though I'm not sure why I would be."

"I know it's a lot to ask, but can you come, please?" she begged. "I could really use your support right now."

She had been really looking forward to spending her first New Year's Eve with Cole, but if she agreed to go to the party, not only could she support Rebekah, she could keep an eye on Granny and Gladys. "Okay," Grace agreed. "What do you want me to do?"

"I'll figure something out when you get there." Rebekah gave her another quick hug, then rushed to the door. "Thanks, Grace, you're the best!"

Grace stood there a moment longer, then decided it was time to go help Granny. After that, she would call Cole and cancel their plans. Good grief, this day was depressing. Which was not at all how she wanted to start the new year.

One-Evening

"You look beautiful," Grace gushed as Granny slowly turned in a circle to show off her new dress and styled hair. Chrissy had stocked some gorgeous gowns that were perfect for New Year's Eve parties and had helped Granny pick out a lovely sequined dress in a shade of green that matched her eyes.

Granny stopped twirling and grinned at Grace. "I feel like a young girl again!" She clasped her hands together and did one more spin. "I better stop before I make myself dizzy," she joked.

"Knock, knock," Gladys called out as she entered Granny's bedroom. "Oh, Josie," she said, stopping when she saw Granny. "You look amazing!"

"So do you!" Granny said as she took in Gladys's similarly styled red sequined dress. "I'm glad you went with the red—you pull it off so much better than I do!"

Grace pulled out her phone and opened her camera app. "You both look stunning! Now, I need you to stand close together so I can get a picture."

Gladys handed Grace her phone. "Can you take one for me, too, please?"

"Of course," Grace said as she accepted the phone. "Say cheese!"

She took several pictures, then winced when she heard the doorbell ring; Vincent and Mitchell had arrived to pick up their dates. Grace was torn. This was the happiest she had ever seen Granny and Gladys, and yet there was a possibility she was sending them off with a couple of con men. Should she try to stop them and ruin their happiness in the process? Or should she let them go and pray she'd be there to stop it should something happen?

If there had been any question in her mind that Granny and Gladys were in physical danger, Grace would have had zero problems intervening. But since she didn't believe Vincent and Mitchell would hurt them, she ultimately decided to let them go and have their night.

"I'll get the door," Grace announced. She bounded out of the room and to the foyer, her nerves increasing with each step. When she threw open the door and revealed the men, both of whom looked sharp in their black tuxedos, a burst of nervous laughter escaped. "Don't you guys look handsome!" she exclaimed, hopeful they didn't notice how awkward she was.

"Still no match for that cowboy of yours, but I think we clean up pretty nicely, if I do say so myself," Vincent replied. He gave Grace a wink, his eyes twinkling with amusement. "Are the gals ready?"

As if on cue, Granny and Gladys materialized behind Grace.

"We're right here," Granny called out. "We just need a moment to put on our coats."

Vincent and Mitchell moved past Grace and into the foyer.

"Here, let us help you with that," Mitchell said as he picked up Gladys's coat and helped her into it.

Once the ladies were ready to go, each man offered an arm to his date.

"Have fun!" Grace said cheerfully. "I'll make sure to check on you a few times tonight."

Vincent's head snapped toward her. "You're going to be there tonight?" he asked.

Grace searched his face. He was smiling, but unless she'd imagined it, there had been an undercurrent of unease in his tone. "I'm helping serve," she replied.

Mitchell and Vincent exchanged glances, but neither said a word.

"I guess we'll see you later, then," Vincent replied. His tone still held a hint of unease, his smile momentarily fading before being replaced with a brighter one.

There was definitely something wrong, but Grace held her tongue. She just couldn't make herself ruin this night for Granny and Gladys. All she could do now was hope that decision wouldn't come back to bite her later.

***

When Grace arrived at the winery, her mouth dropped open in awe; Rebekah had truly outdone herself and was easily on the way to fulfilling her dream of becoming the best event planner in the Midwest.

White lights lit up the tree-lined drive, artfully illuminating the path to the parking area near the large white tent. Outside the entrance to the tent was a large arch decorated with black and gold roses, little lights weaving throughout to add a splash of color. If that wasn't impressive enough, the inside of the tent was a sight to behold.

In the front of the tent stood a platform where a quartet of violins sat playing classical renditions of songs from the sixties and seventies. Long tables lined with golden tablecloths and adorned with black rose centerpieces framed a wooden dance floor, as waitstaff dressed in formal attire weaved through the crowd with trays of champagne flutes and hors d'oeuvres. But the real showstopper was the opposite side of the tent where the table for the anniversary couple was set. A large Happy 50th Anniversary sign hung prominently over their seats, which just so happened to be two large golden thrones. It was tacky, arrogant, and sophisticated all rolled into one.

"Grace, I'm so glad you're here!" Rebekah said as she came up from behind her. "One of the servers called out sick and I need someone to man the drink station." She pointed toward a table in the corner of the room that held a punch bowl and cups, as well as an assortment of soft drinks and teas. She took in Grace's outfit of jeans and a sweater. "Um, I'll have to ask the catering company if they have a spare uniform."

The corner would be a great place to watch the guests from—four of them in particular—so Grace readily agreed, even if she was a tad insulted to once again have her clothing called into question. Though, to be fair, a sweater and jeans did not quite match the aesthetic. She followed Rebekah without question to the kitchen inside the winery and then dutifully changed into the uniform once it was handed to her. It was a tad bit too large, but she figured she could deal with it for one night.

Once she was dressed, Grace took her place behind the table and began to fill the little crystal cups with punch. When that was done, she stood and watched the crowd, her eyes scanning the somewhat familiar faces for Granny and Gladys. She finally spotted them out on the dance floor, laughing and singing along to Etta James's "At Last" as Vincent and Mitchell expertly twirled them around the space. Her heart melted at the sight, and she quickly pulled out her phone to snap a couple of pictures.

"Oh, it's you," Alexandra said as she helped one of her children with a glass of punch. "How many jobs do you have?" She scrunched up her nose, and without waiting for Grace to reply, leaned down to address her daughter. "This is why daddy works so hard," she said as she pointed at Grace, "so we don't end up like her."

Grace leaned over the table and addressed the little girl. "People like me are the reason your mommy doesn't have to work at all. If we didn't exist, she would have to do her own cooking, cleaning, laundry, and"—Grace picked up a cup of punch and lightly tapped it to the little girl's—"she'd have to make her own punch!" She gave the little girl a big smile.

The little girl smiled back at Grace. "Teacher says we should be nice to people or they might spit in our food!"

"That's one reason," Grace said as she gave Alexandra a mischievous smile.

Alexandra's eyes bulged as Grace's meaning became clear. "You wouldn't dare," she spat. She tried to maintain her haughty expression but faltered under Grace's stare. "Come along, Penelope." Alexandra ushered her daughter away, the little girl waving goodbye despite her mother's insistence to ignore Grace.

She should probably feel bad about that, but Grace honestly didn't care. One more day and they would be gone, nasty attitude and all.

At six-thirty on the dot, Alexander and Audrey made their grand entrance into the tent. The quartet played "When a Man Loves a Woman," which Grace later learned was the first song they danced to at their wedding fifty years ago. She had to admit, they were a striking couple. As they made their way to their thrones, someone handed Alexander a microphone, and when Audrey was seated, he tapped on the mic several times to get everyone's attention. The quartet ceased playing, those on the dance floor took their seats, and the servers quietly left the tent, all but Grace, who remained where she was, eager to watch whatever came next.

Alexander pulled a gold rectangular box out of his jacket pocket and placed it in front of Audrey, then turned to face the crowd. "I want to start by thanking all of you for coming out tonight. I will admit this trip has been a little...different than expected, but I appreciate you all being good sports."

As the group applauded, Grace did her best to refrain from lobbing cups full of punch at him. How dare this man insult the very people that made this night possible—and in front of them, to boot. Finding spit in their food was the least of their problems; if they weren't careful, Grace might take a page out of Valerie's book and put a snake in their bed. Okay, fine, she wouldn't actually do that, but the thought was tempting.

"It's hard to imagine fifty years have passed," Alexander continued. "In some ways, it feels like it's been longer; in others, it seems like we just met yesterday." He picked up the champagne glass someone had placed in front of their seats earlier and raised it to Audrey. "Here's to another fifty years!"

Audrey picked up her own glass and clinked it with her husband's as the crowd shouted out things like "here, here," and "I'll drink to that!" For her part, Grace remained silent, her focus on Vincent and Mitchell as she watched for...what exactly? Did she expect them to pull out a pen and paper and convince Granny and Gladys to sign away their rights to their houses then and there? She honestly wasn't sure what she should be watching for; she just knew she couldn't look away. That is, until she heard Audrey gasp.

Grace turned her attention back to the couple and stared in disbelief at the piece of jewelry in Audrey's hands. Apparently, while Grace had been watching Granny's table, Audrey had opened the golden box Alexander had placed in front of her moments before. And in that box had been none other than the allegedly stolen necklace.

"Open the locket, my love," Alexander encouraged.

Audrey did as instructed, then placed the locket over her heart with one hand as she wiped her eyes with the other.

"For those of you who can't see, I updated our photo to a current one," Alexander explained. "Of all the things money can buy, the one thing it can't is love. I love you, sweetheart, now and forever."

A chorus of "awws" reverberated throughout the room as Alexander kissed Audrey's cheek, then helped her clasp her locket around her neck. While she normally would have found this display to be touching and may have even shed a tear herself, Grace found herself seething instead. She was tempted to leave that very minute and lock them out of the hotel for good. Let them see what else money couldn't buy. But that would take her away from Granny, and she wasn't willing to leave her to the mercy of these vultures.

The quartet struck up a new song as the guests went back to their earlier conversations. Soon after, dinner was served, and Grace was free to furiously text Cole updates on how the night was going. She was in the middle of one such update when a shadow fell over her and caused her to look up.

"Ah, Grace, I didn't expect to see you here," Alexander said as he picked up a glass of punch. He tipped it toward her, then leaned in close. "I think Audrey's had enough champagne for the evening. Do you mind making sure her glass stays full?"

"How could you?" Grace asked, her fury rising above her manners.

"Excuse me?" Alexander stepped back, his brows furrowing in confusion. "If you don't want to fill her punch cup, fine, but that's no reason to be so hostile."

Grace tried to take a calming breath, but it came out as more of a snort. "That's not what I'm talking about, and you know it." She studied him for a moment, but his expression never changed. "You're the one who stole the necklace," Grace said in exasperation.

"Oh, that," he said, waving his free hand dismissively. "I knew it would work itself out eventually."

"That's just it," Grace said through gritted teeth, "it didn't 'work itself out.' You allowed an innocent woman to be falsely accused of theft, and that rumor made its way through town. Her reputation has faced serious harm as a result of your actions."

Alexander appeared unmoved. "I'm sorry to hear that. I'm sure once the truth comes out, she'll be fine."

"And if she isn't?" Grace demanded.

Alexander swallowed hard and shook his head. "Look, you don't understand. It was the only way to ensure the gift was a surprise. I'm sorry your friend got caught up in the mess—that part was unexpected—but I never meant to hurt anybody."

"And yet, someone was hurt," Grace pointed out. "The least you can do is talk to Officer Smith before you leave."

"Fine," Alexander agreed. "Now, if you'll excuse me, I need to get back to my wife."

Grace watched him leave, her anger at his carelessness only somewhat abated. He could have, at any point, spoken to Officer Smith privately and explained the situation. Instead, he allowed the rumor of a theft at the hotel to continue without thought or care as to the consequences. She supposed in his world, there simply were no consequences for this kind of thing. That snake was becoming more appealing by the second. Luckily for them, the ground was still covered in snow and the odds of her finding one were slim to none. Also lucky for them, she was afraid of snakes, so even if she did find one, she was more likely to run the other way.

The rest of the evening was uneventful—though why she expected a party full of mostly elderly people to be anything but was anyone's guess. From her vantage point in the corner, Vincent and Mitchell behaved like perfect gentlemen. Did that mean the con was off? Or was it more likely to happen after the party when they took the ladies home? That seemed like the more likely scenario if paperwork was to be involved.

When the clock struck eleven forty-five, to Grace's surprise Derek Morgan arrived, dressed in a tuxedo and carrying a Bible. He grabbed a microphone and cleared his throat. "May I have everyone's attention?" he said as he tapped the top of the mic.

For the second time that night, the quartet stopped and the attendees returned to their seats.

"I've been invited to officiate Alexander and Audrey's vow renewal," he announced.

Alexander offered Audrey his hand, then led her to the front of the table where Derek was waiting.

Grace looked on with the rest of the guests as Alexander and Audrey pledged to love, honor, and cherish each other through sickness and in health. As Derek pronounced them husband and wife, the audience counted down to midnight, Alexander kissing his wife as the clock struck twelve. Even though she was still angry, Grace found their devotion to each other touching. She even clapped with the rest of the guests as they yelled their congratulations.

Soon after, the guests began to disperse. The party was over; it was time to go home. Grace looked for Granny and Gladys, but she couldn't find them anywhere. Concerned they'd beat her home, Grace quickly changed out of her uniform and left as quickly as possible.

Once home, she raced inside, ready to catch Vincent and Mitchell in the act—only, they weren't there. Her thoughts racing a mile a minute, Grace rushed to Granny's room and found her fast asleep. How long had she been there? Grace could have sworn she'd seen her during the vow renewal. Was she going crazy? Worse than that, did that mean Granny and Gladys had already fallen prey to Vincent and Mitchell's scheme?

With a heavy heart and far more questions than answers, Grace quietly shut Granny's door and headed up to her room. Tomorrow was a new day—and a new year. Nothing she could do now but wait to see what they'd bring.

Morning

If Grace got any sleep at all, she didn't remember it. She'd watched in despair as the numbers on her alarm clock counted down one minute at a time until she had to get up and go back to the hotel. Part of her figured she was wasting her time. It was unlikely her guests would be out of bed before ten at the earliest, but there was always that one who surprised her.

Before she left the house, she checked on Granny, who was still sound asleep. The real estate folder was in the same position it'd been the last time Grace saw it, so she was hopeful that was a good sign. Just in case, she'd done a quick search of the living room and dining room but hadn't spotted any unusual contracts lying around. Did that mean they were safe? Boy, did she hope so. But it was equally possible Vincent and Mitchell had taken whatever paperwork there was with them. If there was paperwork. There was still the possibility this was all nothing more than a figment of her overactive imagination.

With that done, there was nothing left to do but go to the hotel and start on breakfast. Her car, however, appeared to have other plans and opted instead to drive in the opposite direction to Cole's. Strange how that kept happening...

Five minutes later, she pulled up to the house and hopped out, her hand reaching for the doorknob just as the door opened, revealing a very handsome cowboy.

"Happy New Year," Grace said as she threw her arms around his neck and breathed in his scent. "You have no idea how much I've missed you."

His arms wrapped around her waist and pulled her tight. "I might have some idea," he murmured, kissing her cheek as he drew her inside and shut the door.

Max and Ruby each let out a bark and jumped out of their beds to greet her.

Grace laughed as two cold noses eagerly pushed their way into her hands. "Hello to you, too," she said, bending down to pet them both. The sound of a faint 'meow' came from the direction of the couch, and Grace hurried over to scoop up Piper and snuggle her face into her fur. "I've missed you as well, little fur ball!"

When Piper had had enough and began to squirm, Grace placed her back on the couch and returned to Cole's waiting arms.

"Any news?" he asked as he rained kisses across her cheeks and forehead.

"No," Grace whispered, leaning in as close as she could. She looked up into his electric blue eyes. "And that worries me just as much."

Cole kissed the tip of her nose. "Whatever happens, we'll face it together, okay?"

Grace rose up on her tippy-toes and kissed him for as long as she dared. She then pulled back and smiled up at him. "I'm sorry we couldn't spend New Year's Eve together. Any chance we can make up for it tonight?"

"Of course, baby," he replied. "We aren't bound to the days themselves, you know. We can celebrate whenever we want to."

She gasped at him in mock horror. "You would dare say such a thing to the queen of holidays?" She made a show of looking around. "What if someone heard you?"

Cole rolled his eyes and laughed. "Go take care of business, silly. The sooner you finish, the sooner you can come back to me."

That was a plan Grace could get behind. She kissed him one more time, then took his hand as they walked out together. When they reached her car, it took all of her strength and willpower to say goodbye and drive away. Somehow she managed, but not without a dozen reassurances she would see him again in just a few hours. She would just have to pass the day quickly. Not a difficult task when she had three meals to prepare and fifty demanding guests.

***

To no one's surprise—especially her own—the guests were all still asleep when Grace finally arrived. Grateful for the quiet solitude, she made her way to the kitchen, turning on the lights as she went. When she reached the coffee maker, she found a card addressed to her sitting on top of it. Confused, she slid onto one of the stools at the counter and opened the envelope.

Inside was a single sheet of paper, the handwriting unfamiliar.

Dear Grace,

I know you know what Mitchell and I were up to, and all I can say is I'm sorry. I know those words are meaningless given the circumstances, but I have never meant them more than I do now.

I wish I had an explanation for you, some reason that if it didn't excuse my behavior, it at least justified it, but sadly, I don't. We do what we do because we can. Because it's an easy way to make a good living. Yes, it's reprehensible; no, I'm not proud of it, but that doesn't seem to be enough to get me to stop.

With you, though, things were different. The setup was the same, the outcome would have been as well, but at some point, I found I was unable to go through with it. Maybe it was all our talks in the kitchen. Maybe it was watching you stand up to my sister and niece. Your spunk and sass reminded me of, well, me. In you I felt a kindred spirit!

Well, this is goodbye, kiddo. I hope somehow you'll find a way to forgive me, but I won't blame you if you can't. Someday, maybe you'll grab a cup of coffee from that blasted machine and think fondly of our time together.

-Vincent

P.S. Josephine and Gladys are wonderful ladies. Do them a favor and find a couple of honest men to take them out from time to time. Not only do these old bones hate the cold, they hate being lonely, too.

Grace wiped the tears from her eyes as she scanned the letter a second time. Yes, she'd been right about everything. So why did it all feel so wrong? Because she'd been fond of Vincent, too. She was going to miss their early morning conversations. Which also felt wrong, given what he'd planned to do to her granny, to her. "People are so complicated," she mumbled.

She called Cole and filled him in, then called Grant and did the same.

"I don't want to say I told you so, but, I told you so," Grace said after reading the letter aloud to Grant and Molly.

"I never said I didn't believe you," Grant replied. "I just said it wouldn't be easy to prove."

That wasn't quite how Grace remembered it, but she was running on nothing but caffeine and day-old muffins at this point, so her memory was shaky at best. "What do we do now?" she asked quietly. "I still feel we should have a talk with Granny and Gladys, just in case the letter is fake."

"Molly and I can handle that at breakfast, if you want?" Grant offered. "It might be a little less, how shall I say, emotionally charged coming from us."

"Are you calling me a drama queen?" Grace accused. Of all the nerve—she was absolutely NOT a drama queen. Why, she was the epitome of level-headedness, and calm, and cool, and... okay fine, she could be a drama queen. "Whatever, just let me know how it goes."

Grant made a noise that sounded suspiciously like a laugh. "Will do."

He ended the call, leaving Grace to sit in the large kitchen in silence. Well, she could cross that problem off the list. So where did that leave her now? There was still the issue with Jilly, but once the events of last night got into the hands of the correct people *cough* Bea, that problem should hopefully resolve itself. That left the issue of Rebekah and Thorne. It may not be her business, but there was no way she was going to allow her friends to suffer one moment longer than necessary. No, she needed a plan. She also needed to make breakfast.

Grace walked over to the fridge and ruffled through the shelves. Were these people a "black-eyed peas and cabbage" kind of people? Probably not, although, to be fair, neither was she. Maybe that's why she always had bad luck.

A thought popped into her head. Since it was unlikely she would see anyone for at least another hour or two, could she get away with serving brunch instead of breakfast and lunch? It would reduce her workload by a third and would give her more time to get operation "get Rebekah and Thorne back together" underway. Hmm, she really needed to work on her creative naming skills.

Now, what should she make for brunch? Egg casseroles came to mind. So did pancakes, French toast, fruit salad, and sides of bacon, sausage, and hash browns. Surely even the queens of mean wouldn't be able to find fault with this.

That settled, Grace went to work as a plan began to form. First things first, she needed to get Rebekah and Thorne together, preferably in a neutral place. She looked around the kitchen. This could technically be neutral ground, though it was also the scene of the crime, so she wasn't sure it would work. Oh well, maybe it would be cathartic to hash things out in the same place they experienced their greatest heartbreak.

Next, she needed a reason to get them to stay. Grace glanced down at the eggs she was beating. A little food never hurt anybody. She could always claim she needed them to be taste-testers or something. Third, well, that part would have to be up to them. She could lead a horse to water, but she couldn't make it drink, as the saying went.

She finished assembling the casseroles and put them in the oven, then pulled out her phone and sent a quick text to Rebekah asking her to stop by the hotel in two hours. When Rebekah texted back a thumbs-up, Grace let out a sigh of relief. One down, one to go. Thorne, however, was going to be a little more difficult to get here.

After a few minutes of debating alternate options, Grace made up her mind and called Thorne. When he didn't answer, she hung up and called again.

"Hello," Thorne said once he picked up.

He sounded awful, and Grace got the feeling she wasn't the only one who'd had a sleepless night. "Hi Thorne, I'm sorry to bother you, but is there any chance you can swing by the hotel in the next two hours?"

The phone was silent for so long, Grace checked to see if he'd hung up. "Thorne, are you there?" she asked once she saw the call was still connected.

"I really don't think that's a good idea," he finally said.

This was exactly what she'd feared. "Please, Thorne, I wouldn't ask if it wasn't an emergency."

That seemed to get his attention. "Emergency?" His voice was suddenly clear and strong. "What kind of emergency?"

"I keep hearing noises in the wall, and I'm concerned there may be an animal trapped in there. Please, Thorne, I'm not sure what else to do." Grace knew she was laying it on thick but hoped to appeal to his knight-in-shining-armor side.

"Okay," Thorne agreed. "But why don't you want me to come now?" he asked suspiciously.

"Oh, um, well..." she hadn't thought about that. "I don't want the guests to know about it," she stammered. "I'm afraid they'll think it's mice and use that against me, you know?"

Thorne was quiet for a moment, then cleared his throat. "It's very likely it is mice," he said. "Not to alarm you, but that's pretty common this time of year. Well, anytime of year in these parts. But I'll come take a look, just in case."

"Thank you so much!" Grace exclaimed. "I'll see you in two hours!" She hung up before he could change his mind. Her plan was actually working; phase one was now complete. On to phase two!

Happy New Year!

Afternoon

Grace stepped back and admired her handiwork; phase two was now complete. It had taken her the entire two hours to cook all the food, set up the buffet in the dining room for her guests, and create this romantic table setting for two in the kitchen. Rebekah and Thorne would simply have to go along with her plan; to do otherwise would be quite rude after all the work she'd done for them.

"I'm here," Rebekah called out as she entered the kitchen. "What crisis do we need to avert now?" she joked. Her smile faded when she saw the table set up in the corner. "What's all this?" she asked suspiciously, her eyes taking in the lit candles, rose bouquet, and setting for two.

Thorne walked in, his face pale, his eyes red, his blonde hair standing on end. He took one look at Grace and Rebekah, then raked his hand down his face. "Well, there's definitely a rat in here, but it's not in the wall."

"Oh look, you're both mad at me," Grace deadpanned. "Now you have something in common to bond over." She walked over to Thorne and began to push him toward the table. Once he was seated, she did the same to Rebekah.

"It's time to put an end to this foolishness," she said sternly. "You both love each other, you both want to get married, so you both need to tell each other how you feel and work this out. You're not leaving this kitchen until you do."

Rebekah gave Grace a sardonic look. "You know you can't really make us stay here," she said sarcastically.

"That is debatable," Grace replied, her voice syrupy sweet. "Regardless, I shouldn't have to. Now eat your food I made with love before it gets cold, and get to the making up part already. I'll be over there doing dishes for the millionth time if anyone needs me."

As Grace walked away, she overheard Rebekah remark to Thorne, "Man, she sure is bossy these days!" She smiled to herself; phase three was close to a success. Tempting as it was to do a fist pump, she worried that might jinx things, so she settled for a baby pump at her side.

Grace had every intention of giving the couple as much privacy as possible, but that was a difficult thing to do when she was sharing the space with them. Sure, she could have put in headphones and turned the volume up loud enough to drown them out, but let's be honest, she was dying to hear what they were saying.

"I appreciate what Grace is trying to do here," Thorne said, his hand waving to indicate the table, "but I'm not sure there's a way forward for us. We can't pretend what happened yesterday never happened."

"No, we can't," Rebekah agreed. "And honestly, I don't want to. I've spent my entire life avoiding the hard conversations, the difficult choices. It wasn't until my parents cut me off that I was finally forced to face things." She paused for a moment and sighed. "When my mom showed up, I think some part of me reverted to the person I was before. I don't want that, and you don't deserve it."

Thorne nodded in understanding. "Losing you is the worst thing that has ever happened to me," he said, his voice gruff with emotion, "but your happiness means more to me than my own." He stood and began to make his way to the door.

Grace was about to launch herself onto his back to stop him from leaving, but before she could, Rebekah called him back.

"Wait," Rebekah called out.

Thorne stopped but made no move to return to the table.

"I don't want to break up," Rebekah said, her voice full of emotion. "I want us to get married, to live in your cute little house together. I want to have kids and a dog and go on late-night client runs to help deliver baby cows and horses." Tears began to stream down her face as she bared her heart to him.

He slowly turned around to face her, his eyes also full of tears. "Then why did you say no when I asked you to marry me?"

Rebekah crossed the room and took his hands in hers. "Because I was afraid the only reason you were asking was to stop me from going to New York."

"I don't want you to go to New York," Thorne stated matter-of-factly. "And I don't want you to marry that Tom guy, or become a socialite like your mother, or whatever else it is they wanted you to do. But I didn't propose to stop you from doing those things, I proposed because I wanted you to know how important you are to me and how serious I am about our relationship." Thorne cupped her cheek with his hand. "I love you, Rebekah."

"Ask me again," she whispered.

Thorne got down on one knee, took both of her hands in his, then looked deep into her eyes. "Rebekah Rutherford, would you do me the honor of becoming my wife?"

Rebekah nodded enthusiastically. "Yes!!" She threw her arms around his neck and kissed him, knocking him off balance so they both tumbled backward. Laughing, they held each other for a moment before getting back up.

Grace wiped her eyes, then handed them each a tissue. "Congratulations!" she exclaimed, giving them each a hug. "Now go sit down and eat your celebratory brunch!"

"Yes, Mom," Rebekah teased. She took Thorne's hand and led him back to the table. "We need to get her off the energy drinks!" Rebekah said in a stage whisper.

"I heard that!" Grace called out as she took another sip of her rocket fuel. Now that phase three was complete, and all was once again right with the world, Grace was ready to get back to the dishes.

There was only one more big meal to go, and Grace wanted it to be special. The relationship between her and her guests—well, really only between her and Audrey—had been strained since day one, and if it was at all possible, Grace wanted things to end on a positive note.

However, there was one thing she needed to do before she dove into the task, and that was confront Granny.

***

When Grace arrived back at the house, Molly, Grant, Gladys, and Granny were waiting in the dining room for her.

"I know we decided you should do this without me," Grace said to Grant. "But I didn't want to be left out."

"I understand," Grant nodded.

Granny gave Grace a quizzical look. "What's this about, dear?"

"Yeah," Gladys chimed in. "We're missing the annual *Star Trek* marathon!"

Grant addressed Granny and Gladys. "We don't want anyone to feel attacked," he began.

"Oh, just spit it out already," Gladys said with an eye roll. "We already know Vincent and Mitchell were trying to con us."

Grace's eyes widened in surprise. "You do?" She looked at Granny. "But you told me—"

"—not to worry about it," Granny finished for her. "Gladys and I have been around the block a time or two; we know when we're being taken for a ride."

"I don't understand," Grace said, completely flabbergasted. "Why didn't you tell me?"

Granny reached over and patted Grace's hand. "You were already being run ragged, dear; the last thing you needed was one more thing to worry about. Since Gladys and I weren't in any danger, we decided to just go with the flow and have a little fun."

"And boy did we have fun!" Gladys exclaimed. "Those old codgers may be slimeballs, but they sure knew how to cut a rug!"

Grant cleared his throat. "I'm glad you two had fun, and I'm even more pleased you didn't fall for their scam, but that doesn't change the fact that there are plenty of other victims out there who did."

"This really pains me to say, but I think we need to continue to investigate them," Grace replied. "The thought of someone else losing their home kills me."

Molly gave Grace a sympathetic look. "First of all, I want to apologize to everyone for going a little overboard this past week—"

"A little?" Grant asked, his brow raised.

She gave him a look, then playfully swatted his arm. "Fine, a lot overboard," Molly relented. "Now that I've gotten that out of my system, I should hopefully handle things better in the future." She paused to give each of them an apologetic smile. "Second, I wanted to update you guys on the business side of things. I've been watching our social media accounts and while there have been a couple of complaints, the vast majority of the comments have been positive. So, good job, Grace!"

"I bet I can guess which guests left the complaints," Grace pouted.

"Don't worry about it," Molly replied, surprising everyone. "A couple of bad comments is actually a good thing. If all we had were positive reviews, people might get suspicious they're fake and deem us untrustworthy. As long as the majority are good, a couple of bad ones could actually boost our overall reputation."

That sounded good to Grace, so she decided to roll with it. "Please tell me we have enough money for me to finally take some time off?" Grace begged.

Molly and Grant exchanged looks. "I can easily give you till the middle of February, but if you want to pay for your wedding, continue making repairs to the hotel, and keep a healthy amount in savings, that's the best I can do. Which means..."

"Cole and I should get married this month?" Grace asked hopefully. Surely now that they had to set a date, things would fall into place and she could finally marry the man of her dreams. Scratch that—she was marrying that man this month come hell or high water. Even if she had to drag him down to the courthouse kicking and screaming. Though honestly, Cole wasn't the one she'd have to worry about—Rebekah and Molly were.

"If you married in, say, three weeks' time, that would give you two weeks for a honeymoon, and then another one to two weeks to get settled before the next Experience," Molly explained.

"I can work with that," Grace readily agreed. "I just need to see if Rebekah can make that work." She checked her watch, saw it was time to get back to the hotel, and stood. "Is that all?"

Molly nodded. "If you need help tonight, I'm free," she volunteered.

Grace could have used her help a long time ago, but decided against saying that. Molly had apologized; that would have to be good enough. "I'm fine, but thanks for the offer," she replied. Grace gave everyone a quick hug, then headed for the door.

"Hey, Grace?" Grant called out.

Grace paused and turned to look at him. "Yes?"

"I just wanted to assure you that we're going to keep working on the stuff with Vincent," he informed her. "I'm sorry it seemed like we didn't take it seriously yesterday."

"That's okay," Grace replied. "Even I wasn't sure I believed me, and honestly, I wish I'd been wrong."

"He must have been quite the character," Molly said gently.

Grace considered that for a moment. "Yeah, he was," she agreed. "But that's not the worst part. The worst part is he genuinely seemed like a nice guy. He even defended me to his sister and niece. If you'd asked me a couple of days ago who the villains in that family are, I would have easily said Audrey and Alexandra. But while they are rude and thoughtless, Vincent and Mitchell are actual criminals. How am I supposed to reconcile that?"

"Sweetheart, he was a con man," Granny reminded her. "Part of his act is to be charming and kind. It's how they lure you in."

Molly looked at Granny in surprise. "How do you two know so much about these things?" she asked Granny and Gladys.

Gladys shrugged. "We watch *Dateline*."

Grace laughed as she shook her head. "You two," she teased. "I better go. Happy New Year, everyone!"

"Happy New Year!" they shouted back.

Evening

This was it—it was time for her to serve the final dinner to her guests. Grace had spent a considerable amount of time planning the menu. At first, she had intended to do another 'fancy' meal, but after a week of doing nothing but that, she decided to do something different and prepare them a genuine, down-home, Midwest-style meal. After all, they weren't likely to get one of those back in New York. It was a risk, especially since Audrey had reacted with disdain to her stew and salad on the first day, but it was a risk Grace was willing to take.

For the starter, Grace prepared baked potato soup. It was warm, hearty, and wrap-you-in-a-blanket-and-plop-you-in-front-of-a-fireplace comforting. It was also delicious, if she did say so herself. Which she did. A lot!

Grace had already set the tables, with the soup bowls on top, so all she had to do was wheel her large pots of soup out to the dining room and ladle a serving into the bowls. When she got to Audrey's table, she received a 'look,' but this time, Audrey kept her opinion to herself.

Once that was done, Grace removed the bowls, then returned to the kitchen for the main dish: pot roast, mashed potatoes and gravy, green beans, and fresh-out-of-the-oven homemade dinner rolls. This time, when she served Audrey, she simply nodded her head in acknowledgment. Was Grace winning her over? Or was Audrey plotting her demise? It was hard to tell, but Grace really hoped it was the former. After all, who could resist pot roast?

As she waited for her guests to finish, she fixed a couple of plates for her and Cole, then sent him a quick text.

I can't wait to see you!

Three little dots immediately appeared, then the following popped on the screen:

Waiting as patiently as we can!

A few seconds later, a picture of Cole, Max, Ruby, and Piper sitting on the couch came through. All but Piper had party hats on, and behind them was a Happy New Year's banner Cole had hung behind the couch.

A huge grin spread across Grace's face. This was the man she was going to marry. God willing, fifty years from now it would be her and Cole celebrating their fiftieth wedding anniversary.

That is the most adorable thing I've ever seen! Don't party too hard without me!

She peeked into the dining room to see if they were done. It would be rude to rush them, but boy, was she anxious to finish up and get home to Cole. When she saw there were several still eating, she sighed and returned to plating the dessert: good old-fashioned peach cobbler and vanilla ice cream. To give it a touch of class, she drizzled the plates with a salted caramel sauce. It was the perfect end to a perfect meal—at least in her eyes.

Before she went out to clear the dinner dishes, she made sure to pack up the extras to take to Cole's. He deserved this meal as much as her guests did for putting up with her craziness all week. And at least Cole would appreciate it; he loved a good home-cooked meal.

Grace took another peek, saw that almost everyone was chatting happily, so she decided now was a good time to clear the plates. Once that was done, she pushed the loaded cart to the dining room and handed out the dessert. This time, when she set Audrey's before her, Grace received the tiniest hint of a smile. Just what was going on here?

Alexandra, for her part, did not look impressed but hadn't complained either. It was practically a miracle!

Since she didn't want to risk spoiling the mood, Grace hurried back to the kitchen and loaded the dishwasher. As soon as the guests finished dessert, she could clear the tables and finally get out of there. The minutes could not pass fast enough.

She was just about to start the first load of dishes when Alexander walked in. Grace took a deep breath and turned to face him, her disappointment hard to conceal. There was only one reason he would come in here, and that was to complain. Her plan had failed; they'd hated her meal.

"Um, what can I do for you?" Grace asked hesitantly.

Alexander cleared his throat. "I just wanted to tell you that was the best meal I've had in a long time; maybe ever."

Grace's eyes widened in surprise. That was huge praise coming from him, especially since he and his wife had just had their big anniversary dinner the night before.

"Wow, um, thank you!" she said, her smile growing as the compliment sank in. She hadn't failed after all.

Alexander continued to stand there, a sheepish look appearing on his face. "I also want to apologize for the mishap with the necklace. As I said last night, it honestly never crossed my mind any harm would come from that little incident." He cleared his throat. "And I wanted to let you know I personally spoke to Officer Smith and explained the whole situation," he informed Grace. "He was also not very happy to have wasted time on a non-event, but he has closed the case."

That was good to know. Hopefully it was enough to clear Jilly's name, but in a town this small, full of people who love to gossip, Grace wasn't so sure. Eventually people would move on, but Jilly could still be in for a rough few weeks.

"Thank you," Grace replied again. "I don't believe I had an opportunity to tell you this last night, but Happy Anniversary, and Happy New Year! It's inspiring to see a married couple make it to fifty years. I hope my fiancé and I will one day follow in your footsteps."

He eyed the engagement ring on Grace's finger. "Thank you, Happy New Year to you, too. And best wishes on your upcoming wedding!" Alexander nodded, then returned to the dining room.

Grace watched him leave, the tension in her shoulders lessening by the second. She'd done it—she'd managed to make peace with the Bellamys. All it took was homemade pot roast. Next time—and she really hoped there wouldn't be a next time—she would start with that.

***

By the time Grace made it to Cole's, the caffeine from all the energy drinks she'd drunk all day had worn off, as had the high from serving the best meal her snooty guests had ever eaten. Simply put, she was exhausted. However, that would not stop her from spending the evening with Cole. She'd just have to chug another can or two... or three.

Cole met her at the door, the dogs anxiously waiting behind him for their turn for pets and treats. "I swear they miss you as much as I do," he chuckled.

"I miss them, too," Grace said as she rubbed their bellies. "I'm counting down the days until we can live together under one roof."

"Oh?" Cole raised his brow. "Does that mean you've made a decision on where we're going to live? Or have you finally decided on a wedding date?"

Grace looked up at him in surprise. "Of course I wouldn't make such monumental decisions without you. I'm just tired of living separately from you and all our pets." She looked back at Max and Ruby. "And we need to set a date for some time in the next three weeks," Grace mumbled.

Cole leaned against the wall and crossed his arms. "I'm sorry, what was that?"

She turned her head so he could hear her better. "I said we need to set a date for some time in the next three weeks," Grace repeated.

"And why, may I ask, are you mumbling that?"

"Because I don't want whatever it is that's cursed us to hear me say that," she replied.

Cole snorted and helped her to a standing position. "We are not cursed, silly. We just had a string of bad luck, that's all."

"Even if that's true, I'd like that string to end," Grace said as she looped her arms around his neck. "I mean it, Cole, I'm not waiting any longer. Either we have the wedding, or we go to the courthouse."

He leaned down and kissed her—gently at first, and then with a lot more passion. Eventually, he ended the kiss and led her to the kitchen to heat up their meals. "How about the third Saturday this month?" he suggested. "That should give Rebekah plenty of time to put something together, and us plenty of time to decide where we want to go for our honeymoon."

"Sounds good to me," Grace replied. She then paused in the middle of scooping the mashed potatoes to look at him. "Did we just set a date?"

"I believe we did," Cole confirmed. "How do you feel about that?"

How did she feel about that? It wasn't like it was the first time they'd done so—more like the third or fourth. But this time things felt different. It felt right. She repeated the date a few times in her mind, and honestly, it had a nice ring to it. This was it, this was the day they would finally get married—she could feel it.

"I think I better let Rebekah know," Grace told him. "However," she said, putting down the spoon and wrapping her arms around him, "right now I'd rather focus on you."

Ding!

Grace jumped at the sound of the microwave finishing. "I guess the pot roast is done." They finished fixing their plates and moved to the couch in the living room to eat. Grace admired the banner he'd hung, then looked over at the tree to see Piper sleeping on the bottom layer of branches. "I see you lost the war," she joked, gesturing toward the cat.

"We've come to an understanding," Cole said cryptically.

"And what understanding is that?" Grace asked as she tried to hide her smile behind a spoonful of green beans.

Cole gave her a sheepish look. "Piper gets to sleep in the tree and I let her."

Grace laughed. "Oh, Cole, you are going to be such a pushover when we have kids!"

He set their plates down on the coffee table and pulled her onto his lap. "When we have kids, eh?" he asked as he nuzzled her neck. "You certainly are full of surprises tonight." When she let out a giant yawn, Cole stopped and studied her face. "Baby," he said softly. "You look positively exhausted."

"I don't care," Grace said as she snuggled against his chest. "I already missed celebrating with you last night—I am not missing tonight, too."

"How about this," he proposed, "we'll pretend it's almost midnight, make a toast, and then you'll go straight to bed." He put his finger against her lips when she opened her mouth to protest. "No buts, young lady. Don't forget you still have to get up in the morning and make breakfast."

Dang it, he was right. She would also have to clean all the rooms, wash the bedding, and clear out all the perishable food so it didn't go to waste. "Fine," she reluctantly agreed.

Cole gently moved her back to her seat, left the room for a moment, then returned with two champagne flutes and a bottle of sparkling cider.

"What should we toast to?" Grace asked as he handed her a glass.

"Hmm, how about, to new beginnings?"

Grace smiled and raised her glass. "To new beginnings!"

They clinked glasses, then sealed it with a kiss.

"Happy New Year," Grace murmured against his lips.

"Happy New Year, baby girl."

The Next Morning

Epilogue

Morning came way too early. The countdown to her wedding was about to get a lot shorter because, after this, she planned to sleep for an entire week. On second thought, maybe she should sleep for all three weeks. Then she could skip all the wedding drama and show up when it was time to walk down the aisle. Nah, who was she kidding? If there wasn't drama, could there even be an event? It was like that old saying about the tree falling in the woods.

Somehow, she managed to get out of bed and make it to the hotel on time. Since the guests would be traveling that day, she decided to make it easy for them—and her—by providing foods that were easy to take on the road. Such as donuts, muffins, bagels, and all things that came from Bea's Bakery so Grace didn't have to cook.

Check-out time was officially eleven, but Grace was at the front desk and ready to usher people out at six. Plenty of people had flights to catch; with an hour-and-a-half drive to the airport, they needed to get on the road as soon as possible. One such family was Alexandra, her husband Preston, and their three young girls.

"I hope you enjoyed your stay!" Grace said brightly as she accepted their room key.

"I suppose it was fine if you prefer trailer-park chic."

That was actually nicer than Grace had expected, so she let it go and focused on the kids. "Goodbye, Penelope," she said, waving to the little girl.

Penelope's face lit up and she beamed at Grace.

Alexandra rolled her eyes. "Let's go." She grabbed Penelope's hand and dragged her toward the door. Her husband and sons followed without question; none of them uttering a word.

Grace shrugged and helped the next person in line. Around thirty minutes later, Rebekah strolled in.

"Perfect timing," Grace informed her. "This is the first break I've had all morning."

"Sorry, I planned to get here earlier, but I overslept."

"No worries. You didn't have to come at all. Which brings me to my question: why are you here?"

Rebekah laughed. "I figured I owed you some help after everything you went through this past week; especially since you did it for me."

"I'll never turn down help." Grace's tone was serious. "Oh, since you're here, Cole and I set a date. Three weeks from this Saturday."

"Um." Rebekah pulled up the calendar on the computer. "I can make that work."

They looked up as Audrey and Alexander approached the desk.

"Rebekah!" Audrey exclaimed. "It's lovely to see you again. I didn't think I was going to get the opportunity to say goodbye."

"Thank you again for trusting me with such an important celebration." Rebekah extended her hand.

Audrey shook it and nodded. "It was everything I hoped it would be."

Grace smiled and extended her own. "I hope you enjoyed your stay!"

"It was... quaint." Audrey shook her hand. "The next time either of you are in New York, give me a call and we'll do lunch."

Alexander nodded. "Ladies." Then he followed Audrey to their car.

"Do you think she meant it?" Grace asked once they were out of earshot.

"Meant what?"

"That we should do lunch?"

Rebekah snorted. "Of course not; that's just something we say to people—typically the ones we have no intention of ever seeing again."

Grace shook her head. "Y'all are a strange bunch."

"How dare you include me in that group," Rebekah said in mock indignation. "From now on, I am Midwestern proud!"

Grace raised her energy drink. "I'll drink to that!"

Rebekah snatched the can and held it out of reach. "No more of these, silly. By now, you've probably had enough caffeine to stop an elephant's heart."

When a few minutes passed and no one showed up to check out, Grace checked the computer and saw that everyone had left. "Guess it's time to start cleaning."

They looped their arms and headed toward the supply closet.

"So," Grace asked as she pulled on her rubber gloves, "how does it feel to be engaged?"

"I'm not sure it's sunk in yet. We're supposed to go ring shopping this weekend, so I suppose it might feel more real then."

Grace wheeled the cart out of the closet and double-checked their supplies. "So when's the big day?"

"Geez, Grace, one wedding at a time!"

"We could always do a double wedding. That could be fun!"

They wheeled the cart down the hall.

"How about you let me worry about the wedding stuff; you focus on becoming the future Mrs. Grace Reed?"

"Party pooper!" Grace stuck her tongue out, then erupted in giggles when Rebekah rolled her eyes. She hugged her friend, pulled the master keys out of her pocket, and opened the door. "After you," she said, sweeping her arm toward the room.

A flash of white drew Grace's attention. On the dresser near the TV sat a white envelope with her name scrawled across it. When she picked it up, she heard the sound of metal clinking. Intrigued, she opened the envelope, turned it upside down, and two quarters landed on her palm. Apparently, Audrey had taken Grace's comment about tips to heart.

"What's that?" Rebekah asked.

Grace held up her palm. "My tip from Audrey."

Another fit of giggles burst forth, and by the time they were done laughing, they were both on the floor, backs against the bed.

"Hey." Rebekah scooted a few feet and grabbed a piece of paper off the floor. "Looks like this fell out of the envelope." She handed it to Grace.

Grace flipped the paper over to reveal a check in the amount of one thousand dollars. She looked up in surprise. "I guess she didn't hate me as much as I thought she did after all."

Rebekah put an arm around her shoulders. "Oh, Grace, I don't think it's possible for someone to hate you. Believe me, I tried!"

Grace playfully shoved her, then helped her to her feet. "Alright, let's get to work. These rooms ain't gonna clean themselves!"

"Yes ma'am."

Rebekah saluted and went to work stripping the bed while Grace emptied the trash. The New Year's event was over; she and Cole had finally set a date, and the countdown to their wedding had officially begun. If Rebekah hadn't stolen her drink, Grace would have toasted to new beginnings again!

Afterword

Dear Reader,

Thank you so much for reading this book, I truly hope you enjoyed it!

I would like to start out by giving a special thanks to Angela Ratliff for generously sharing some of her ideas with me for this book! It is due to those ideas that Granny and Gladys had something more to do than just provide gossip and a friendly ear for Grace, and I love that for them! I think moving forward there will be a lot more hijinks in store for those two!

Up next is Countdown to a Wedding! I am so excited to finally give Cole and Grace that special moment, but you know there's gonna be some more drama along the way! I also have plans for Jilly to get her own spin-off series and that will be coming soon. Then the sequel to Hope Blooms in Willow Glen.

Thank you for coming along on this journey with me, Cole, Granny, Gladys, Rebekah, and the rest of the gang. It is you, dear reader, who makes Winterwood special, as without you it would be nothing more than an empty town.

-Dianna

P.S. If you'd like to join my newsletter you can do so at diannahouxshop.com :)

www.ingramcontent.com/pod-product-compliance
Lightning Source LLC
Chambersburg PA
CBHW032232050726
47591CB00001B/358